LOVE

and

Other Criminal Behavior

Stories by

Nikki Dolson

BRONZEVILLE
— BOOKS —

To CBVB

ISBN: 978-1-952427-00-8
Library of Congress Control Number: 2020938395

Stories previously published: Georgie Ann (*Bartleby Snopes*, 2015); Take the Hit (*StoryGlossia*, 2009); Stars (OneTitle, 2012); The Mistress (*Tough*, 2019); How to Be Good (Back Alley, 2009); Hello, My Name Is Denise (*Front Porch Review*, 2012); On Monday Nights We Danced in the Park (*Day One*, 2016); Laundry (*Red Rock Review*, 2007); Mendelson in the Park (*Red Rock Review*, 2015); Our Man Julian (*ThugLit*, 2015); 83 (Shotgun Honey, 2017)

Bronzeville Books Inc.
269 S. Beverly Drive, #202
Beverly Hills, CA 90212
www.bronzevillebooks.com

BRONZEVILLE
BOOKS

CONTENTS

Georgie Ann . . . 1

Take the Hit . . . 9

Stars . . . 19

The Mistress . . . 33

How to be Good . . . 37

Sunrise . . . 59

Hello, My Name Is Denise . . . 71

On Monday Night We Danced
        in the Park . . . 83

Laundry . . . 107

Mendelson in the Park . . . 117

Lucy Lucy Lucy . . . 127

Our Man Julian . . . 145

83 . . . 163

Georgie Ann

Georgie Ann is dead. Her husband and all of our crowd around her coffin. They stand with their backs to us and their arms thrown over each other's shoulders. We, the dutiful spouses, black suited and Prada heeled, sit waiting for our cue to cry.

The casket is open. We've all done our viewing, and we agree she looks great for a dead woman of her age. She is ten years our senior. Was.

One of us says what we're all thinking, "How much hairspray do you think they used? Her hair never held curls like that."

"Maybe it's a wig," another says. We contemplate this. Georgie's bangs are perfect, her face looks flawless, and her head is tilted on the pillow to smooth out her neck wrinkles. Her crow's feet are hardly noticeable.

We were not Georgie Ann's friends. Not really. Though our husbands, all former college football players now golfers with love handles and bald spots like medieval monks, are the best of friends. Greek letter brothers till the end. We spouses did not like each other, but none of us liked Georgie Ann, and in that, we found friendship.

We are our husbands' equal opportunity, Rainbow Coalition of spouses. Their Generation X Stepford Wives. They chose well. We represent their America: Liane is Japanese American. Oscar is Mexican American. Jodi is from New York. I am the black, Midwestern ex-cheerleader (truth be told, we are all ex-cheerleaders), and Georgie Ann is our brown-sugar-haired, southern Barbie doll. Together we've endured birthdays, anniversaries, and rotating dinners at each of our homes. And always, we suffered Georgie Ann, but I swear we didn't kill her.

Georgie Ann's husband begins sobbing loudly. Oscar stands and offers his pristine white handkerchief to his husband, the tax lawyer, who mouths thank you and gives it to the crying man. After our fight and weeks of not talking to me, Oscar sits down next to me and takes my hand. I lean against his shoulder. Oscar and I are friends, real ones.

Liane and Jodi and Georgie Ann live next door to each other. Their spacious houses all in a row. Each with matching tennis courts and pools and gazebos, like they all went to the same architect and said, Give me what she wants. Oscar and I live across the street and sometimes feel a world away from them. We have no pools or gazebos. We make do with multidirectional showers and sunken bathtubs. His house is a two-bedroom, faux English-style cottage; mine is a three-bedroom, Spanish tile–floored Frank Lloyd Wright knockoff. Our lots are a third the size of theirs.

The funeral director asks everyone to take their seats. Our husbands sit together in one row, and we sit in another, united. Georgie Ann's husband doesn't make eye contact with us. He stands before the assembled mourners and praises his wife's good works. Her volunteerism. Her saintly mothering of their children, who spent the school year at boarding school and were never actually at home.

Tears slip down his clean-shaven cheeks. He places a hand on the coffin of our Saint Georgie Ann.

———•—•—•———

Georgie Ann was fifty-one years old, but from the neck down, it seemed as though her body had stopped aging at thirty. Two children nearly wrecked her, but a team of doctors rebuilt her better than she was before, complete with a new bionic hip. From the collarbone up, though, Georgie looked every year of her age. To combat this, she wore scarves around her neck to distract from the turkey-wattle thing that was happening. Her bathroom was a department store of face creams. When we came to visit, the four of us would discuss her new acquisitions like swooning teenagers discussing the football captain. It seemed she single-handedly kept infomercials on the air with her purchases of each buying of the next new thing. She'd seen a documentary once about plastic surgery gone wrong and liked to cited Jennifer Grey as a reason not to put your face under the knife. "You can't tell who she is. No one calls her 'Baby' anymore. Her career is over, all for want of a nose." We all nodded and agreed, because when Georgie Ann was right, she very was right. Then there were the other times, when she said things like:

To Liane, during her first pregnancy, "Lamaze is for wimps."

And to Jodi, "Natural childbirth birth is the only way to go."

To Oscar, "You still don't want to actually get married? Now really, is a civil partnership going to take care of you when you're old?"

And to me, "Aisha, have you seen the watermelon at the farmers' market? It's divine."

This is Georgie Ann. Was. This was Georgie Ann.

———•—•—•———

Georgie Ann died in her kitchen. It was the last barbeque of the summer, and she was hosting. She was also angry. While we three of us stayed outside with the husbands, Georgie Ann and Jodi went to finish the deviled eggs and pull the steaks for the grill. She told Jodi, in between licking the deviled egg spoon, that her husband, the Silicon Valley software developer she seduced when she was thirty-four and he was twenty-four, was cheating on her. Again. This time she was filing for divorce, Georgie Ann had said. Then she grabbed the steaks off her marble counter, plastered on a smile, and sauntered out onto the patio in her pencil skirt and red-soled, five-inch heels. The rest of us were in jeans and T-shirts. Georgie Ann never dressed down. She was always on.

When we left Georgie Ann laid out on a chaise lounge fanning herself and came into the house to cool off and reapply bug spray and SPF, Jodi told all, and we said, No shit, with straight faces. Oscar cut a look at me. He knew things the others didn't. He knew that I was the one sleeping with Georgie Ann's husband.

I did not intend to have an affair. Oscar had been telling me for months to end it. He warned, "One of you is going to slip up. Then I will have to choose sides, and my man will want me to drop you. I don't want to have to break up with you." His husband thinks Oscar is always on the verge of leaving. Oscar would live in the gutter if that were the only way to keep his husband. His love has no end. No situation would cause Oscar to ever do to his husband what I have done to mine. This is what we fought about. We were supposed to have lunch one day, and instead of meeting him, I met Georgie Ann's husband at a hotel. It wasn't the first time I'd done it. An hour after my forgotten lunch date with Oscar, my phone held six text messages and eight voicemails from him. I called to beg forgiveness as I reapplied my lipstick.

"Where the hell are you? I thought you were dead somewhere," he said. He was in the bathroom at his office. His concern echoed off the walls.

I giggled, then straightened. "I forgot about lunch. I'm sorry."

"Are you going to answer my question?" He was suspicious now, and I couldn't lie to him. Not to Oscar, who stroked my hair after my miscarriage. My Oscar, who on Halloween let me dress him up as Freddie Mercury while I went as Prince, much to our husbands' dismay. The others refused to do more than hand out candy. Georgie Ann turned off her lights, put her two yapping terriers in the yard, and pretended not to be home.

"He called," I said, wincing when Oscar began cursing. I didn't know what he said, Spanish was his swearing language of choice, I took French in high school, but I got the gist. "Oscar, I'm sorry. I'll make it up to you."

"Don't bother," he said, and hung up.

Oscar thought I was risking too much, but I couldn't help myself. Georgie Ann's husband was the fitter, less bald version of my own husband, and he was better in bed. My lover didn't call me Aisha, but A, spoken *A*, said like a prayer or a note in a song. When we met in hotel rooms, he'd say "A, let me see you," and I'd undress. Each time, I'd stand there, naked in front of him for a moment, feeling glorious under his gaze, then he'd press me up against the door and run his mouth over me. Over every inch of me. Like he couldn't get enough. My husband seemed to have had enough of me by year ten.

When Georgie Ann's husband sold his company three years ago, she had wanted him to move the family to Europe. I was the one who convinced him to start a publishing company. Now he published six books a year. All of them reprints of classic pulp-era books that now got him write-ups in the *Wall Street Journal* touting him as the anti-Jeff Bezos. He was saving the written word. He kissed me last December in Jodi's garage when we were supposed to be finding her spare tree lights. Our attraction only grew, but we were content to keep things as they were. We lived less than fifty yards apart.

———•●•———

We were all married the same year, fifteen years ago. Liane in March. Jodi in May. Oscar was our June bride, and Georgie Ann waited until September, right when autumn was settling into fall when the leaves were at their most vivid color. Not long after, my husband, the civil engineer, and I got drunk and eloped in Reno. When we woke to rings and hangovers, we decided to stick it out because all his friends were married, and he didn't want to be the first to divorce. I was a writer and didn't make any money at it, and he promised to support my dreams. We did not understand each other's jobs in the world, but we were content to coexist in our ignorance.

Let it be said that we tried to be happy. On our first anniversary there was torrential rain. My husband drove us out to a project site where we stood and watched the street fill up with water and slowly creep up the sidewalks, crest over the landscape and trickle into the parking lot. He pointed at the rushing water, dirty and swirling, and said, "You're like the water. Terrible and beautiful and necessary." If I had ever doubted that I loved him, those doubts were gone in that moment. It's funny the things you forget.

———•●•———

Georgie Ann's death came during dessert. We spouses went in with the dirty dishes and left the husbands on the patio to bullshit and smoke the Cuban cigars that Jodi's hotel developer husband had scored. Liane is pregnant with baby number three and is nauseated by the smell of fresh-cut grass and any kind of nicotine-laced smoke.

That night it was my turn to bring dessert. I brought a cheesecake

I said I made from scratch, but really it came from a local bakery. Georgie Ann pulled out another bottle of wine. I rooted around in her kitchen drawers to find the pie knife. She stood behind me, close as a lover, and put her hand in the drawer with mine. She came up with the corkscrew triumphantly, scraping up my arm with the sharp metal point as she did. I yelped. She said, "Sorry, doll." Our gazes locked and I knew she knew.

Liane and the others sat down at the breakfast bar while Georgie Ann poured the wine and I served cheesecake.

"Can I have just water?" Liane said, sounding tired. Her baby is a nonstop mover, and she hasn't been sleeping well. Georgie Ann tutted and poured Liane's wine into her own glass and downed it in three gulps. I found a tumbler and bottle of water for Liane because she was afraid of the minerals in the tap water. "Is it cold?" she asked. I told her I'd put ice in it, and she nodded. Georgie Ann scoffed. "The ice is filtered tap water. What exactly is the difference?"

Liane only shrugged and rubbed her protruding belly. She's a slim woman, all baby in front now with only a few weeks to go.

"Leave her alone, Georgie Ann." I pressed the tumbler against the lever for the icemaker and filled it. When I turned around, Georgie Ann was in my face. "Don't tell me what to do in my own house." Her nose and cheeks had gone red from alcohol.

I stepped around her and set the glass on the kitchen island's imported-marble top. "Relax, Georgie," I said, making a face behind her back. The others saw it and smiled private smiles, except for Oscar, who frowned behind his wine glass. I poured the water into the glass and moved to give it to Liane, but Georgie Ann was right there again. This time she knocked the glass from my hand. It shattered on her travertine-tile floor, and water soaked us both from the knees down.

"You think you can just come in here and flaunt yourself in front of him?"

I took a step back. I saw Oscar stand. "Georgie Ann," I said. She came after me, her manicured hands reaching for my hair, for my throat, for my face.

Whether it was ice or glass she stepped on, I don't know. One minute she was bearing down on me, the next she was lurching left, then right, her heels slipping on the tiles. The back of her head hit the corner of the island top, then she was on the ground. Motionless. A broken thing. I knew this instantly. Then she was a curiosity.

We just looked at her.

It was quiet, save for the low rumble of Liane's husband's laugh coming in through the open French door. Then Liane said, "Oh, there's blood," and clutched her belly.

Jodi said, "What was she talking about?"

Oscar said, "Is she?"

I prodded Georgie Ann's leg with the toe of my sneaker. The body rocked slightly, but there was no rising and falling of perfect C-cup breasts under her cashmere tank top. Jodi stepped forward, curious. Oscar reached for my hand. Together we watched the blood spreading from her head mingle with the water on the floor and turn into a bright, red halo.

The husbands walked in, laughing, and, seeing us, asked what we were looking at. We spouses jumped. Then one spouse pulled out her mobile and called 9-1-1. One burst into tears. One consoled the other. Another spouse hugged their husband and told him what happened. It was an accident, we said. Later, the husbands will think we're hiding something. But it happened just like we said. Only we didn't mention the long minutes we watched her dying on the floor. Or that we all thought, If it had been one of us, she would have poured herself another glass of wine. That was Georgie Ann.

Take the Hit

Kendra "Black Bear" Hayes was backed against the ropes and getting worked over by Athena "Titan" Dulane, a five-foot-ten blonde batterer who was nine years younger and six inches taller. Athena was a rookie keen on making a name for herself and using Kendra as the punctuation. Kendra's gloves were up high in a wasted effort to protect her face. Soon—very soon—her opponent was going to make her promised move, and that broad, flat forehead of hers, the one she tried to cover up with teased and hair-sprayed bangs when she was outside the ring, was going to come down like an anvil on Kendra's face and down she would go. Match over; TKO. Takethehit-takethehit-takethehit was Kendra's new mantra. She winced when the next fist landed, her breath stuttering out. Maybe the money wasn't worth it after all.

Kendra and her opponent were the opening act for the main event: two local boy fighters from neighboring cities. Their hometowns' high school rivalries would be resolved by the outcome of their fight. They were fighting in an overly warm, old high school gymnasium, and the matches were the building's last event. Over

Kendra's head, the school's old basketball banners hung limply from steel support girders. Next week the gymnasium would be demolished, making room for an ethanol company's expansion into rural Illinois.

Again Athena's fist connected with Kendra's side, an earthquake rolled through her torso. Where's the goddamn bell? Take. The. Hit. Kendra pushed off the ropes, delivering two quick punches that made her opponent lean her long torso away and step backward. Athena recovered and returned with her own combo, slower than Kendra's. Keeping up her end of the deal, Kendra allowed the last punch, a weak left hook she'd seen coming, to glance off her jaw. She staggered back against the ropes, sliding left a couple of steps. The blow had stung, but useful things are often painful. She'd only needed a moment to see the room.

To her right, past the table of three perspiring judges in suits, were rows of men in folding chairs. The men, all standing up, some of them drunk, were yelling: Fight! Fight! Fight! She'd spotted Maury's red-headed self, standing in his cheap navy-colored suit, next to the double doors that led back to the gymnasium's locker room. She'd seen the referee, a bearded, beer-gutted man who likely refereed based on his betting tendencies, leaning back in the opposite corner of the ring, his head turned toward Maury. She'd seen enough to understand. Maury was holding up the bell. Either that, or time itself was running in reverse. No way was two minutes this long. Her arms were getting tired from the weight of the borrowed, 16 oz. gloves, from having to hold back her natural aggression, from ignoring her gut instinct to beat her opponent to her knees, then spank her like the baby she was. Only twenty years old and Athena thought she knew everything. The gall of her to show up in Kendra's bar talking trash, trying to push her buttons to get Kendra to fight.

"Nobody would blame you for being gun-shy," Athena had said, after bellying up to Kendra's bar like she belonged there. As if her being there was an everyday occurrence. "Your last fight with Adams was a battle, that's for sure. You went five rounds before she took that low blow. You were lucky that head-butt of hers missed."

Athena took a sip from the bottle of beer she'd asked for. Kendra had done her job and served the girl. It wasn't in her job description to talk to the customers, so she hadn't said anything, only looked up at Athena from behind the bar and tucked one of her many braids back behind her ear. She waited for the girl to say something that mattered. Athena set the bottle aside, leaned over the bar, and told Kendra, with a smile that some might mistake for kindness gracing her pale face, that if she got in the ring with her, Athena wouldn't miss.

Kendra had smiled back, full and unflinching. She kept smiling until Athena's own smile weakened. Athena backed out the front door. The three regulars in the bar, old men retired or fired from the steel mill or the Caterpillar factory and who knew Kendra used to box, raised their drinks in a toast to her and said, "Bring back the Bear!"

Kendra was often thought to be too soft, even for a woman, to be a boxer. Her face was round, and her nose was small and turned up a little at the end, her eyes full and friendly. An old boyfriend called her face "cherubic." An ex she didn't talk to anymore likened it to a dog's, all cute and playful until the fangs came out. Kendra was partial to that description. Back then she'd be a dog or a bear or whatever it took to win. Now she'd do only what was necessary.

———•———

Athena, it seemed, was in love with punching Kendra's torso now, tagging her repeatedly on one side, then the other. She swung a wild punch at Kendra's head. Kendra dipped and shifted her stance. She felt the rhythm of the fight settle over her, like always. Often Kendra felt energized, almost euphoric, this deep into a fight. The natural beat of the moments between the bells. She'd find a second wind, and it always propelled her to victory. But today was different. She wasn't here to win. Her ears were hot from the glancing blows, and sweat ran between her breasts. She paced her breathing to the blows, waiting for the bell. Waiting for Maury to be a stand-up guy and not still be all about the money. She wasn't feeling pain, exactly, only the thud of blows given and received. There was a dull throb in her head. One of Athena's punches had connected and driven the beads woven into Kendra's braids deep against her skull. She felt her ponytail loosening, and a twist hung limply behind her ear.

Someone yelled, "Kick her ass!" and Athena grinned down at Kendra.

"Hear that?" Athena said, coming closer, her voice muffled and distorted by her mouth guard. "Gonna do that. Gonna fuck you up."

She reached for Kendra, trying to corral her into a corner. She wrapped her long arms around Kendra. Instinctively, Kendra's head went down and pillowed against Athena's chest. In the clinch now, they both delivered ineffectual punches into each other's sides. Kendra knew Athena was waiting for the ref to pull them apart, then she'd deliver the promised head-butt.

Kendra decided she wouldn't take another punch. She was all alone in the ring. Maury wasn't thinking of her or Athena. To hell with taking a fall. She still felt ill at the thought of lying down for this chick, this wannabe boxer.

———•—●—•———

When Maury called a week after Athena's visit, she should have hung up on him, but he'd asked the right questions at the right moment: How much for you to fight again? How much more for you to lose? She'd gone home that night to her empty apartment and figured out what it was worth to her to get back into the ring.

Kendra left boxing after she had found out she was pregnant. One day she'd been a boxer; the next, she'd been a retired one. It'd been so easy to trade one life for the promise of another. Could she do it again? In her closet was the baby book, with all its brief memories: the sonograms and a lock of newborn hair and a card from a fertility clinic in Chicago received three months after the funeral. She decided that night she could do it again. As long as Maury met her price: twenty thousand dollars, more than enough for two in vitro fertilization treatments. With what was left of the twenty, combined with the money she'd been saving the three years since her baby died, she'd have enough to be fat and pregnant. No need to work and no struggling to pay the bills for over a year. So she'd agreed, and now she was getting bruised by a woman with a weak left hook. Fuck that.

————•————

Kendra earned the nickname "Bear" because of a low growl that would rumble up when she was angry or frustrated or just for the hell of it. Now, as Athena lifted her right arm to deliver another punch, determined to pound Kendra through the mat and into the concrete foundation, Kendra growled low and shoved forward, masking her planned move within another. Athena's right arm flailed momentarily. Kendra took a half step back, curled in on herself, planted her right foot, and popped her head up and into Athena's chin, snapping her head backward. The other boxer took one step back, blinking at the steel ceiling.

Kendra hesitated, part of her wanted to rush in, to finish her off. Part of her wanted to bend down over a semiconscious Titan and say, "I live for this shit. Didn't you know? This is why I'm on this earth. To fight you and put you in your goddamn place." But Kendra held herself in check, watching Athena take one step forward. She watched her hands come up like she was readying herself to punch. Athena's body automatically remembered the stance. That kind of muscle memory came from real work. Maybe Kendra had underestimated her. In the time it took to blink her eyes, Kendra pondered this. Then Athena's head tilted back down, her mouth slack and her eyes nearly crossed from the chin blow, and Kendra hit her.

She jabbed, striking Athena's face: once, twice. Kendra's right fist was pulled back just waiting for its chance. Athena stumbled, and Kendra went for it, an uppercut that cut Athena down. She stepped into the punch, her own grin spreading across her face because it felt good to land a blow with all her strength and desire behind it. To not just punch at Athena but through her. Kendra imagined her fist exploding through a window, pounding through a wall, demolishing steel with that fist. Take this hit, rookie.

The referee rushed over, pushing Kendra away. Athena was face down until the ref hit three in his count, then she moved and rolled over. She stood shakily, took a step, and careened over to the ropes. Athena shook her head. The ref was in her face trying to assess her. Athena pushed him away. Not bad, Kendra thought. All that mouthing off had convinced Kendra that Athena was weak. But maybe she wasn't. The bell sounded. Athena was guided back to her corner.

In the locker room, after the medics looked them both over, Kendra was stretched out along one of the bolted-down wooden benches, feeling the heat leave her body. Where the heat remained, in isolated pools across her torso, the bruises rose like bread. She would be incredibly sore tomorrow. Kendra was waiting for Athena and Maury to finish arguing. Their argument was low and buzzing, Maury's sharp pointed sounds and Athena's furious responses. Athena was angry she'd won by decision, angrier still because now she knew that Kendra had been going light on her and that, for all practical purposes, Kendra had let her win.

Kendra sat up and rolled her head and her shoulders. Maury was looking up at Athena and edging towards the locker room door. Athena was matching him half step for half step. Her hair was slipping out of its French braid, wild strands looking electrified by her anger. The blonde hair framed her ever-reddening face. Athena stuck a long finger at Maury. He flinched. Kendra almost laughed out loud.

"Hey, Maury, give us a minute," Kendra said. The blonde glared at her. Maury, not the fool so many claimed he was for backing female boxers, took the proffered chance and slipped from the room. Now it was Kendra and Athena, with only the lone metal gurney the medics had left behind between them.

"You didn't beat me," Athena said. She fingered her bruised jaw. Kendra shrugged. She stood and stepped onto the bench. Athena moved away from the door and toward Kendra, stopping once she reached the gurney. She put her hands on the gurney's cushion and began twisting the thin sheet that covered it. "Rematch in six weeks."

Kendra shook her head. "Don't be mad because I beat you to the head-butt. Everyone would have seen you do it. You would have looked bad. This way, I'm a bad fighter. You got what you wanted. So did I."

Athena looked down at the gurney. Kendra saw a shudder go

through her. Athena's voice was low and strained when she said, "I didn't get what I wanted."

"You beat me."

"By decision!" Athena flung the gurney away. It crashed into the end of a row of lockers, metal against metal ringing and sounding the bell if Kendra were game. Athena was clearly up for it. Tears welled up in her eyes. Her fists were balled at her sides. She turned her body sideways, readying herself. "I had you."

Kendra wanted to tell her she never had a chance. Kendra had fought better and bigger opponents than her. Athena was so young, so foolish, so full of herself. She was ripe for Maury's brand of manipulation. Kendra remembered well what being his girl was like. All the shine and glitter he'd wanted to sprinkle over Kendra to make her into a face instead of a boxer. "You're too pretty to box," he'd said a hundred times. To the point that when she did finally get hurt—a cut over her left eye that later matured into an impressive scar—she'd been ecstatic. Finally, she'd earned a mark to signify she was a serious boxer. Maury had teared up at the sight of the stitches for nearly a week. Maury wanted her to wear bright colors and push-up bras. He wanted her to flaunt her sex around the ring instead of concentrating on her boxing talents. Looking at her replacement, victorious but disappointed, Kendra couldn't help being thankful she'd gotten away from Maury.

Kendra said to her, "Your left side is weak. You telegraph all of those punches. You're like a goddamn atlas. You could be better than that." At the moment she said it, Kendra knew it could be true. She had a flash of Athena fighting and winning against some new female Leonard or Frazier. "Work on that, or the pros will demolish you, and Maury, he'll have moved on to the next girl before you've even realized it."

Kendra hopped down and grimaced. She was stiff. She wanted a shower and her bed. She picked up her gym bag, slung it over her shoulder, and walked past Athena. The boxer made to move after Kendra, but Kendra held up her hand, "We're done."

"I had you," Athena said to Kendra's back. She walked out of the locker room.

In the hallway leading back to the ring, Kendra heard the next event gearing up. The men were entering the ring. The audible wave of support from the crowd rolled down the hallway. No mocking, some trash-talking maybe, but those boxers, those men were respected for what they did.

Maury was waiting for her farther down the hall, by the double doors that led out. "You weren't supposed to try to win," he said, when she got near enough to hear him.

Kendra shrugged. "I made it look good. Besides, I got tired of being your punching bag out there. She still won." Kendra stepped around him and headed towards the double doors.

"Want to come back? After that performance, I don't know if she has what it takes to last out there," he called after Kendra.

"Come back to you? Never. But she'll go the distance."

Kendra walked the few feet to the double doors and hit them hard. The doors squealed open and clanged against the metal jambs as they swung closed behind her. She pulled her hair free of the rubber band and shook her head. Using both hands, she massaged her scalp as she walked to her car. The sun hadn't been down long, and the air was still warm.

Kendra opened the car door and tossed her bag onto the passenger seat. Upon impact, the bag's plastic zipper split open; her street clothes and one boxing glove bulged from the opening. Everything slid to the floor. She sighed, sat down in the driver's seat, and leaned over to push her clothes back into the bag. She winced and sucked in a breath with the motion. She sat up, pulling the glove free as she went. Kendra turned the glove over in her hands, letting her fingers follow its curves, noting the dings and scratches on its dull red surface. She'd need at least a month for the bruises and pain to fade. But she'd deal with that and then schedule her appointment at the fertility clinic in Chicago. And in a year, Kendra figured, she'd have everything she wanted. She exhaled a long, slow breath, then tossed the glove over her shoulder and into the back seat.

Stars

I couldn't find Benny after the fight. He'd left the ring and made his way through the crowd, all of them patting him on his back and shoulders, and he was headed in our direction. I only looked away for a moment to talk to one of his cousins, turned back, and he was gone. I told his father to head on out; I'd drag Benny home soon enough. I watched as his father and the cousins ran for their cars through an onslaught of January rain.

I checked the other locker room for Benny and with the janitor, as he folded chairs and swept the floor of the small gym we were in. Grudgingly, I spoke to Cooper, making sure I smiled a sincere fuck you at him. He shook his head and said, "No hard feelings. I'm sorry I had to drop the kid." He put an arm around me. I shrugged him off and snatched Benny's money from him. Part of me wondered if he dropped Benny because I'd picked him up one night after the bar closed, but I figured Cooper was too keen on a payday to let the personal get in the way of business. Whatever. I wasn't worried. Benny'd find a new manager, or I'd manage him myself. Benny was twenty-seven. His career wasn't over yet.

Benny's disappearing act wasn't new. He had trouble getting the fight to drain away. Sometimes he needed a few moments alone to get his head right. The last time was in Reno. I found him three blocks from the event site watching a Ferris wheel go round and round. He dragged me into a seat, wound himself around me, and spent the next three orbits kissing me, arms tight around me like he was trying to absorb me.

Tonight, I found him outside wearing only his shorts and shoes, broad shoulders hunched and bare under the cold January rain. His head hung down; hands curled in loose fists at his sides. I snagged a garbage bag from the janitor's cart and went out with the bag canted over my head. I got right up under his nose and hollered over the thunder, "Baby, come inside before you catch pneumonia."

Benny tilted his head down. Rain dripped off his face and onto mine. The one eye he could still see out of blinked at me slowly as if he was processing my face, not sure of what he was looking at, and I wondered if I should take him home with me or to the ER. I wondered how well the ring doc had looked him over, but Jimmy knew I'd kick his ass from one side of town to the other if I caught him treating Benny like something less than gold.

In the space between lightning and thunderclap, Benny said, "I'm quitting." My heart did a little stutter beat. Benny and boxing were a good match if ever there was one, and the idea he'd give it up was a bit crazy.

I ignored his statement. I was cold. He had to be colder. I said, "Inside." Benny nodded. It took another roll of thunder before he moved. Benny pulled me to him and moved us inside the gym.

"Shower, babe," he said, his voice a low murmur. I led the way, him a step behind. His teeth were chattering by the time he was naked and in the shower. I added cold medicine to my grocery list.

There was a knock at the locker room's door and a loud "hello" that could only be Cooper. I left Benny in a cloud of steam and quick walked over to the door, because the two of them didn't need to see each other, and if he riled Benny up, it could be murder.

"What?" I said as I closed in on Cooper, him hanging half into the room, grinning at me as if we were something more.

He put a hand up to quell the temper he saw in me and stepped fully into the locker room. He handed me a small plastic bag with gauze, tape, and butterfly bandages in it, all stuff I had at home, left over from my own days of needing it.

"Jimmy figured you might need extra."

I nodded thanks and turned away. His voice was soft as he said, "Hey." A reminder of the other Cooper, the one whose company I had enjoyed for the better part of a year, before I grew tired of his attitude. Cooper was driven and ambitious and never cared who he hurt along his way to becoming great. He had stars in his eyes and wanted the attention money, and notoriety could bring him. I turned back to him, and he came forward, pulling an envelope from the inside breast pocket of his gray suit. "There was a side bet on how many rounds it'd go. I won. That's Benny's share."

I flipped through the bills, counting out five hundred in tens and twenties. "Does he know about this bet?"

"I made a bet on your behalf. You got a future to think about now." He reached out to touch me. I slid back a step.

"I'm not your concern," I told him, and shoved the envelope into my back pocket.

"I'm not allowed to care?" He opened his arms wide, to hug me or maybe just remind me of what I had given up. Cooper in his nice suit. Cooper living in the nicer house. Didn't I remember all the nice things Cooper could give me?

I shook my head. Cooper said, "Look, Benny's not a star. He had a moment, but he's on his way down."

I heard the shower shut off. "Leave." I hurried back, hoping to cut off Benny. He was still in the showers, leaned up against the half wall, skin scrubbed pink.

"Forgot my towel," he said. I found him a towel in the linen closet and waited for him in front of his locker.

Benny dressed, then straddled the wooden bench, his face turned up for my inspection. The eyebrow that always bled wept a little blood now, the right eye was nearly swollen shut, the lip could use a little attention. There was a cut on his cheek, but it looked pretty good. Overall, Benny looked exhausted. He put a hand on my belt buckle and pressed his fingers under the hem of my T-shirt, a soft touch against my stomach.

I said, "Want to go home with me?" His gentle smile was answer enough. I took him home, where I had planned to feed him soup and the last of my prescription Tylenol 3, then put him in my bed where he could sprawl out and rest his sore muscles. I'd be on the couch. Lately, I'd slept better there than the bed. Each morning I'd woken up with both hands pressed against my stomach, as if I was trying to hold the baby in.

Benny had other plans. He sat me on the couch, made me the soup, and tended to his own aches and pains while I ate. I considered telling him about the money Cooper gave me, but I saw no point in upsetting him. He and Cooper were done. We were both done with Cooper.

"I need to provide for you and the baby. This isn't the way anymore." He lifted his fists. I wasn't sure what to say to that. We weren't married, and I didn't expect him to take care of the baby or me. I didn't have a say in his fighting or not fighting. A fighter puts their body on the line every time they get in the ring. If Benny had decided enough was enough, it was. "Besides, much more of this, and I'm gonna look like my dad."

His father, Artemio, had been a boxer until a heart attack made him trade in his gloves for the blue work shirts and slow life of a postal worker. One ear was cauliflowered; one eye never quite kept up with the other. Both hands ached no matter the weather.

"I doubt the baby will care what you look like, just so long as you're around," I said. He took my bowl, rinsed it, then came back to me with the T3 bottle. His right hand gave him problems from time to time, so I opened it and shook out two for him. He swallowed them, then proceeded to strip me of jeans, shoes, and socks.

"Really?"

He nodded. "I'm really gonna lay you down and talk to the baby."

"Get the ice first," I said.

He did then position the not quite six-foot length of his body between the back of the couch and me, his head pillowed on my chest. I the ice against his swollen eye and fell asleep with his outstretched hand warm on my belly, listening to his soft whispers of future plans. Two months later, in March, I miscarried.

After, Benny drifted one way and me another.

———•◆•———

It was through a boyfriend that I found boxing. Because of him, I went inside my first gym. Because of him, I had a strong desire to experience being the one throwing the punches instead of receiving them. I was nineteen. We didn't last long. The boxing did. Once I figured out that I could channel my fear into my fists and defend myself, I was hooked. Then I figured out you could make money at it if you were good. And how I wanted to be good.

Nine years I fought. I won and lost and loved every minute of it. Then I came up pregnant just before a fight. A surprise, but what surprised me more was how much I wanted her. So, I got out of boxing. I lost her five months in. After that, I spent my earnings on IVF treatments, which failed. I gave up. Moved to Vegas. Found some fights. Met Cooper. Broke up. Met Benny. Then I came up pregnant. I thought my luck was changing. Silly me.

———•—•——

In midsummer, Cooper came to visit me where I tended bar. I poured him two fingers of whiskey. He wanted to know if I'd go three rounds with him.

I eyed him. He stood a foot taller than me. "You've got the longer reach," I said.

"True, and I outweigh you."

"But I'm younger and quicker. You'd never see me coming."

"Sweetheart, all I do is watch you. I'd see you coming." We smiled at each other. He drank his whiskey, and like that, we were back on.

I moved into his big house on the hill, a pre-housing-boom score, and I enjoyed his glorious pool and played the dutiful girlfriend. I wore the heels, cooked the dinners, smiled the smiles. By October, I remembered why we'd broken up before. But as a favor to Cooper, I pulled out my old gloves and agreed to an exhibition fight against his newest boxer, Amy Jean Ruggiero. It was decent money, and I'd need the money if I were going to make a clean break from Cooper.

At the event, held in a carnival tent a couple hours drive from Las Vegas, I saw her. At twenty-four, she was eight years younger than I was and acted even younger. Her black hair was done up in twin ponytails that bobbed with her every move. She was talking up a local reporter and blew me a kiss when she saw me. I headed into my changing area, a far corner surrounded by heavy canvas with a bench, a table, and my trainer, Wilson, waiting for me.

As I entered the room, I said, "She does know I plan to hit her, right?"

Wilson laughed. "Yeah, but not too hard, okay? Cooper doesn't want her hurt." He shifted on the bench and grimaced. "Hey Kendra, you think he's doing her?"

I blinked at him, because up until that moment, I hadn't considered the possibility. I nodded, and Wilson made an unhappy grunt. He finished taping me up and laced me into my gloves.

Into the ring we went. Amy Jean punched me. I punched her. The bell rang. We stepped apart to return to our neutral corners; she threw a bullshit punch that landed me on my ass. Exhibition over. The ref kept me from bouncing her head off the nearest turnbuckle. I was dressed and ready to leave by the time Cooper showed up, begging forgiveness. I said, "Sure, no problem, but if I catch her on the street, I'm kicking her ass." Then I left. Outside the tent, Benny was waiting for me, a smile on his face and a butterfly bandage over his eyebrow, telltale sign of his renewed fight career.

"Thought you were out."

"I could say the same about you."

We walked toward our cars, and behind us, I heard Cooper call my name, but I didn't turn around. Benny and I talked six months of nothing over diner coffee and eggs. He told me about his upcoming fight. I told him I'd be there.

Cooper was waiting for me at the house, sitting at the breakfast bar with the pieces of his Glock spread out in front of him, gun oil at the ready. It was a thing he did when he was angry. He said it helped calm him down, but I knew it was just a power play. The guns only came out when the person he was angry with was sure to appear. He looked up from the gun barrel in his hand.

"You hungry?"

"No. You?"

He said he could eat, and while he finished cleaning and reassembling his gun, I turned on his sleek range top and made him a steak slightly burnt, as he preferred. He asked for onions on his steak. I did as asked. I pulled half an onion from the fridge, got the cutting board, and knife from the block. I heard him get up as I cut and tensed waiting for him to do what he usually did when I was at the sink. Hands would slide over my hips, and he'd pull me into him, a kiss to my neck and teeth on my earlobe. Something about kitchen work made him horny. I was deciding if I'd let him when his hands clamped on to me and yanked me from the sink. The knife flew out my hand and clattered across the counter.

He spun me around and slammed me back against the refrigerator. A hand closed around my throat before I could stop him. He squeezed and pressed up. He leaned in close, had me on tiptoe, tears leaking from my eyes. His breath rasped in my ear. He said nothing while I swung and kicked at him. I realized I could still breathe, so I calmed down. Let go his forearm and put a hand on the counter next to me for support. I felt the knife blade with the tip of a finger and inched my hand that direction. Then I waited.

"He talk you into leaving me?" he said finally. His eyes were closed, and his face had gone splotchy and red.

I breathed shallowly for a breath or two. "He told me about his fight coming up. That's all. Not everything is about you Cooper."

It was his turn to take a breath. Then he let me go. That was Cooper, all menace and no balls. When he stepped back, I saw his eyes flicker over to the counter, to the knife I'd wrapped my fist around. Its angle told him all he needed to know.

He sat the dining room table. I served him his steak. He ate and watched me while I detailed how I was leaving him. How I thought we weren't going anywhere, and how I knew he knew it too. He nodded. Chewed. He didn't mention Benny again. I should have been suspicious of that, but I was too focused on Cooper to think of Benny right then. I stayed that night, knowing that trying to leave while he was riled up would be a mistake. Through the night, Cooper walked the house like some restless beast, his footsteps heavy. He'd make a circuit of the house, then stop in front of the guest bedroom's door. He put his weight against it as if he was testing it. I sat on the bed, listening to him. The knife on the nightstand and one of the many guns he owned on the comforter between the door and me.

———— ·•· ————

Benny's fight was a week after I moved out of Cooper's place. The fight was at a local gym, a couple hundred people in attendance. I sat three rows back, dead center. On the other side of the ring was Cooper, hair slicked back, jaw clean-shaven, all business and no charm in sight. Benny flashed his blue mouthguard at me in a smile. He went eight rounds with a guy from Texas. They traded blows until Benny landed an uppercut that had the Texan stumbling on his feet. The ref called it. Benny was victorious. Cooper was gone.

For ten minutes, I waited in the locker room for Benny. Then I went looking for him. Back by the ring, his new manager was in discussion with the gym's owner. I saw Cooper in a throng of people, grinning like he'd won, his hair mussed. Windblown. Then I thought of Benny standing in the rain, so long ago now. A shiver of fear ran through me. I went out a side entrance.

A storm was brewing in the distance. Far enough away to be just a band of dark clouds in an evening sky but it was definitely coming. I was running before I realized it, Benny's name on my lips. I rounded the side of the building and, in a stretch of dark shadow, sprawled against the chain-link fence that surrounded the building on three sides was Benny, one hand gripping the fence, the other low on his belly. I knelt beside him and pulled his fingers away. Blood oozed from a wound. I couldn't tell how deep or how bad it was. I pulled my cell phone out and called for an ambulance, then I pressed my hands over his belly and heard him gasp. His nose looked broken. Blood ran thick and dark over his lips. My poor Benny. He put his hand on my cheek. It was sticky and warm.

"Shh," he said.

I realized I was talking. A string of nonsense interspersed with No and Please.

"Shush, babe," he said again. My vision blurred, and his thumb wiped away my tears. In the distance, we heard sirens.

"I missed you." He grimaced, and I adjusted my hands, pressing in harder.

"Cooper and I broke up," I said.

"Good," he said, spa in pain.

Paramedics found us and pushed me out of the way. They assessed him, pushed him up on a gurney and into the back of the ambulance. I followed them to the hospital, one hand on the wheel, the other dialing his parents.

He was in surgery by the time they showed up, cousins in tow. His mother, Maribel, took one look at me, my hands still red with Benny's blood, and wailed into Artemio's chest. He held her while I explained, with as little detail as possible, how I'd found Benny.

Artemio looked at me, his eyes roaming over me. He sat his wife down in a waiting room chair, told cousins Inez and Tomas to sit with their tía. To me, he said, "Let's get you cleaned up."

He steered me to a single-stall bathroom, locked the door, and pulled handfuls of paper towels from the dispenser. He ran the water in the sink until it was warm, then proceeded to wash the blood from my face. He'd never been sure of me. He chose polite distance over the affection his wife favored me and all of Benny's former girlfriends with. Benny said his father wanted him to marry a particular kind of woman. Someone like his mother: devout, Catholic, with hips made for bearing children. I had the hips at least.

I studied Artemio's lined face, the drifting eye and the thin mouth. I liked the look of Artemio. I told him the truth.

"It was Cooper," I said. His mouth went tight, and he dragged the paper towel over my cheek harder than necessary. I told him what I'd left out before; the gut feeling Cooper had done something. "I can't prove it."

"I believe you."

Tears welled up. I nodded once, then turned to the sink and ran my hands under the flow. I watched the water go red, then pink, and then run clear. I scrubbed with the available soap; the chemical foam bubbled up and covered my hands. I scrubbed at the blood beneath my nails, then up to my forearms, rinsed and repeated. Benny's father stopped me when I reached for the soap a third time. He put his hands on my shoulders and said, "Does Cooper have security in his big house?"

— • ● • —

When he told Maribel we were leaving, she didn't acknowledge her husband, only wrung her hands and rocked while Inez rubbed her shoulders, whispering to her in a low roll of Spanish. She stayed with Maribel while Artemio, Tomas, and I drove to Cooper's house.

At the house, I could hear Cooper's stereo playing some eighties hair band he was fond of still. Tomas entered the house through a back window and opened the French doors for us. They moved through the house ahead of me, directly toward the source of music. I hung back when they walked into his office. I heard his incredulous "Artemio?" and scuffling. There was a thud and the sound of flesh

•29•

against flesh, a punch and a corresponding thud of a body hitting the floor.

"My son," Artemio said. His voice shook. I imagined him glowering at Cooper, eyes narrowed and fists clenching. Benny had the same look right before the bell.

I heard someone spit. Cooper said, "What about him? He won tonight. I lost a grand because of him."

"You stabbed him."

"What? No way. I never laid a finger on your kid."

I walked into the room. Cooper stopped talking. He was on his knees, wearing just his boxers and a white T-shirt. Tomas had his right arm bent up and back with a hand on his shoulder, applying pressure. It shouldn't have been possible for Cooper's face to go redder, but it did.

"Hello, Cooper," I said.

"Sweetheart, what did you tell them?"

"Why?" I squatted down to look him in the eye.

"I didn't do it," Cooper said. Tomas pressed harder. Cooper yelled.

"Did you just watch? Tell them who hurt Benny, and they'll let you go." I kept my voice soft, a caress, and touched his face.

"Get him up," Artemio said.

I stood up and walked back out of the room, my heart hammering in my chest. In Cooper's living room, I sat on his couch, put my head between my knees, tried to slow my breathing, and thought of Benny.

Benny in the ring, sweaty and determined. And Benny in my bed, sleep warm and curled around me. Benny on our first date, the two of us on our backs in the bed of my truck watching airplanes take off and land at McCarran. Benny, pointing out stars in between the planes coming and going, telling me, See that bright one there? That one is for you, then kissing me for the first time.

Artemio touched my shoulder. "Time to go." I nodded and reached between the couch cushions, digging briefly before my hands found the gun hidden there. I put the gun in my waistband and pulled my jacket over it. Artemio looked intrigued but said nothing.

In the car, Tomas was going to drive, and Cooper, hands secured behind his back with duct tape, was in the passenger seat. Artemio buckled him in and slapped his cheek, then he sat behind Tomas, and I was behind Cooper.

"Where are you taking me?" Cooper asked.

"To the desert, I think," Artemio said. "We will wait for Maribel to call us. If she says Benny is dead, you will be too. If he lives, so do you, though you will need a cane to walk from now on."

We were quiet as Tomas drove us toward Primm. Then Cooper decided to start running his mouth.

"Tell me, sweetheart, did Benny really think the baby was his? I mean, you went from me to him so damn quick I doubt you know for sure whose kid you were having." He craned his head back and looked at Artemio. "You can't believe her. She has ulterior motives. She's pissed because I didn't want the kid."

I glanced at Artemio. His gaze never wavered from Cooper's face. My hands trembled when I pulled the gun out. "How fucking dare you?" I pressed the gun barrel into the back of the seat and had a vision of the bullet exiting Cooper's chest and the resulting bloom of red across his shirt.

Then Artemio was on me, one arm pulling me into a fierce hug, his lips at my ear. "Relax. Shh," he said, sounding so like Benny it broke me.

"Please tell me you aren't going to let him go." I sobbed into his shoulder.

Artemio took the gun from me and sat back. "My Benny likes you. He speaks well of you." He turned to look out the window.

It was full dark now. The storm I'd noticed earlier was closer now. Lightning cut the sky on his side of the car. On my side, the sky was still clear, and the first stars were out.

"Do you love my son?"

"I don't want him to die." His face was in shadow. I couldn't tell what he was thinking.

He looked out the window again. The gun was a dark presence in the car. I came slowly to the realization that if Cooper was worth killing for hurting his son, I was too, for causing the hurt. I realized I didn't much care what happened to me. I looked out my window for that one bright star and thought about Benny.

The Mistress

I am the mistress. See me lurk in the near dark. See that man walking into the suburban dollhouse—the guy in the good suit with the well-trimmed beard that is softer than you can imagine—he used to be mine.

He hasn't seen me yet. I'm parked a half block down the street. If he were to look this way, though, he would recognize me. I'm not in a wig or dressed in cat-burglar black, head tucked into a balaclava. I'm in that blue dress he likes. The gun, a Beretta subcompact (a gift from a different boyfriend), is in my purse. The only concessions I've made to my task are the kitten heels I'm wearing. They have bows on the back. I check my lipstick and hair in the visor mirror and smile. If I get caught, I'm gonna look good for my mugshot.

See the mistress kill time by swiping left on the dating app she met him on. I see men hugging women in their profile pics. Couples looking for thirds. Men writing about wanting a long-term relationship but still listing casual sex under wants.

Left Left Left

Mr. Adulterer's profile had none of these things. There were only two pictures of him, each showed off his sweet smile and intense gaze. I got chills looking at his picture.

You're beautiful, he wrote to me. Gorgeous lips. I would like to do things to you. But first, you should let me buy you dinner.

So I did. Then I let him take me to his hotel room where he unzipped my blue dress, then contorted my body in all the best ways. He is a talker. It was how he spoke to me, his voice low and smooth, that did me in. I felt the reverberation of his sound in me for days after.

He severed contact with me three weeks ago.

——— • ● • ———

It's full dark now. His street is empty. All the luxury vehicles snug in their garages. Teacup dogs and the wives who own them all drugged for the night. Often we met at his house. Glorious afternoons spent in each other's company, thrilled by the possibility his neighbors might see us. Sometimes we met in hotel rooms on the Strip. Rarely, we met at my apartment downtown. He didn't like my place. "It's too . . . something." He meant it was too me. All my dresses and heels and pinup-girl style. I should have known he was about to end things.

I am the mistress. See me make to his house, peek through the windows, and gaze into darkened rooms. His is a dollhouse of perfection. Everything just so. But a doll is missing. Where is his Mrs.? I wonder if she's left him. She did sound upset when I called her this morning. Upset, but not surprised. All that matters is that he's home alone right now.

The house doesn't have an alarm, but it does have a broken lock on the sliding glass door. He didn't fix the lock because his wife nagged him about it. "As soon as she stops, I'll fix it. Fifteen years of marriage, you'd think she'd know me. She doesn't get me at all, baby. Not like you do." Then he pushed me to my knees. Mr. Adulterer likes his mistress on her knees. I wonder how much time the Doll has spent on her knees in her perfectly appointed home. Did the cold seeping up from the kitchen-floor tiles make her knees ache like it had mine?

I wonder how he will look on his knees.

———— •●• ————

I am the mistress. See me move silently from room to room on a path of artfully strewn rugs. I loop the kitchen twice and run fingers down the marble counters. I caress the stainless-steel appliances. I peek at the laundry room. I wonder about the stack of half-folded towels. I decide the Doll has left him. I nearly giggle but refrain. I wonder what he will say when he sees me.

I stop in the dining room and admire the cherry wood table with its eight place settings. Hundreds of dinners were eaten here while Mr. and Mrs. feigned happiness. I wonder how long he was married before he stopped being happy with her. I wonder if it was longer than the four months it took for him to get bored with me.

I hear a noise and press myself against the china cabinet, purse clutched to my chest. I hold my breath and listen. Again the sound. Panting? Like someone exercising, maybe? Mr. Adulterer suddenly worried about the extra pounds? Or perhaps he's found a new playmate. I think of his last email to me after I begged to know why we were over. He wrote, It was just sex, baby, and you looked like you could use the attention.

I can't wait to give him some attention.

———— •●• ————

I pull the Beretta and move quickly into the living room. The noise stops and so do I. It's dark except for the television, which is on but muted. The back of his favorite chair is in front of me. His hand dangles off one side. I step onto the hardwood floor. My kitten heels tap-tap-tap as I walk around the chair, but he doesn't say a thing.

"Hello, love," I croon as I walk around the chair, then stop. She rises from her knees, leaving the knife protruding from his belly.

I am the mistress, come face to face with the Mrs. The television bathes us in an awful light. She is speckled with blood from pale face to bare feet. Her ballerina bun is perfectly messy. She folds her arms over her chest.

"You won't need that," she says, eyeing my gun.

I look at him. If I ignore the blood, he seems like he's sleeping. I wonder why I don't I feel sad. "I guess not," I say.

She reaches out and pats my bare shoulder, her fingers still slick with blood. "Let's have a drink."

How to be Good

As they lowered Tonya's husband into the ground, the wind shifted and drew the smoke from her father-in-law's cigar across the grave to her side of the funeral tent. She looked up and met his gaze. He was surrounded by the family men—his two brothers and their sons and, directly behind him, his remaining son, the loyal one, and another six or seven people that Tonya vaguely recognized. On her side of the tent, there was only the funeral director. Just like her wedding, her family hadn't come.

Her father-in-law, Michael, nodded at her. She looked away and focused on the coffin. It was more in the ground than out now, and its sleek exterior reflected the gray clouds overhead. It was made of mahogany, its interior lined with champagne-colored silk. Sam had never liked the feel of silk, not for a shirt and most definitely not for his bed. Tonya had found this out the hard way. He'd complained long and loud when she had made the mistake of bringing home a set of silk sheets, a gift from her mother. She'd given them to their neighbors the next day and lied to her mother every time she talked to her. Sam was more of a cotton kind of guy. When she'd asked if there was some other fabric she could use, the funeral director had spluttered an answer that was more sales pitch, so she gave in to stop him from talking. She was too tired to argue over a dead man's bed. Now she regretted it. Champagne silk? she thought. Sorry, Sam.

When the gears that lowered the coffin had stopped their clicking, Michael stood up, grabbed a handful of dirt, and threw it into the hole. The gesture was so violent that Tonya flinched. He saw it, and he opened his mouth to say something, but the wind kicked up stronger, making the funeral tent flap and a folding chair tip over in the back row. He shoved his cigar into his mouth and moved away from the hole, his brothers tight to his side. She stayed where she was, watching the people as one by one they dropped handfuls of dirt into the hole. The funeral director touched her elbow.

"Shall I walk you to your car, Mrs. Goodheart?"

Tonya shook her head and gently pulled away from his grip. She didn't look in the hole, just like she hadn't looked at his body earlier, at the viewing. She hadn't needed to see her husband dead and didn't need to see the depth of the hole he was buried in now. She'd seen him alive for three years, and she'd imagined him dead in the coffin of her choosing for days now. She didn't need or want to see anything more.

She was halfway to the car, parked strategically away from the rest of Sam's family, when she saw a black Cadillac driving slowly, too slowly, down the lane that led out of the cemetery. She heard footsteps behind her, pounding on the grass, gaining on her. She felt a hand close around her arm, and she stopped, started to turn around, then felt a body press against her own.

"Hey, Tonya."

It was David, Sam's twin and the loyal son, his voice smooth in her ear. Sam weighed thirty pounds more, and the weight had rounded out his face; David was lean, all sharp angles. Tonya always felt the urge to feed David when she saw him. Soften him up; make him a little less hard. Mostly, though, when she saw him, she felt guilty.

"I don't have anything to say to him," she said.

David's arm looped around her. She stood still against him. His chest was hard and unyielding. Sam's body always seemed to envelop her when he hugged her.

"Dad just wants to see you and for you to be a part of us."

"Sam didn't want to be around your father. He had his reasons." Tonya glanced over at the Cadillac.

"Those reasons were between Sam and my dad. It doesn't have anything to do with you."

She could smell David. Sam had worn the same cologne. "Everything to do with Sam has to do with me." She pulled away, walking fast to her car.

"You're a Goodheart, Tonya." David called after her.

She didn't turn around. She thought of Sam and how often he had said the same thing. He'd said it when they were trying to get pregnant. Sam was a Goodheart, so there was nothing he couldn't do. Not quite the truth, as it turned out.

Before she could get into her car, the Cadillac pulled up alongside. She could make out the shape of a head behind the tinted glass. The window opened slightly, and a stream of smoke escaped. Then the car pulled away, stopping briefly to pick David up, then continuing down the lane.

She got in her husband's Buick, started it, and rubbed her hand along the bench seat, wishing he were the one driving her home. She was too tired. She checked her cell phone and saw the missed phone calls, all from her mother. She'd call her mother back later. Maybe next week. Maybe never.

She put the car in gear and pointed it home. Instead, she drove to the house where Sam died.

The house was a large fifties-ranch style. Large trees draped the house in shadows. The grass needed a trim, but it was a healthy shade of green, as were the weeds that grew in the cracks of the concrete path that led to the front door. She walked up to the front door and rang the bell. She was nervous standing there, exposed. She'd spent only a few minutes planning her lies while the Buick's engine ticked and cooled.

Two minutes went by, then she heard someone. The door opened. The owner, Fred Andrews, stood before her in high-waist shorts, a thin white undershirt, and sandals. He was in his late-sixties, pale and wide bellied with thinning hair dyed black.

"You're here to see the house? Come in."

She hesitated. She hadn't expected an invite in. She figured she'd have to work to make it over his threshold. Small favors. She assembled a smile for him and strode in as if she knew what he was talking about.

"Sorry." He gestured to his attire. "I was out back in the yard. Let me give you a tour."

A large hallway led from the front door into the living room. Another hallway went left, and the rest of the house opened up to the right. The house had light-colored wood floors set diagonally. Just like the wood paneling was set in the living room. The furniture was a hodgepodge of red and green: plaid pattern on the couch, teal green on the club chairs, and a four-by-six, forest-green color-block painting that hung on the wall. A brick fireplace painted white sat between two large windows that looked out on the backyard. Off the living room were the dining room and the kitchen, all within view of the living room. Deeper back, he told her, was the garage and the laundry room. Nothing seemed out of place.

"That's the garden there." He pointed out the window. She looked.

All she could see was a lot of green: green grass and a patch of dirt under a very large tree. She nodded.

"I'll be honest with you. I've had a few lookers, but no offers yet."

"You're selling the house?" She couldn't help herself.

He cocked his head to one side. "Yeah, isn't that why you're here? My wife doesn't want to live in a house where someone has died."

"Where did he die exactly?" Tonya kept looking around the room, waiting to see the evidence of Sam. Some intuition about where he had been when he died.

"I didn't get your name."

She looked him in the eyes when she said, "Tonya Goodheart."

His mouth drooped open.

"I don't want any trouble, Mr. Andrews. I only want to see where he died."

He closed his mouth and pointed to a spot behind her. "In front of the couch."

Tonya moved closer to the couch. She saw the floor had a slight discoloration to it.

"I took the varnish off the floor trying to get all the blood," he said.

She shivered. She crouched down and reached out her hand to touch the floor. Her fingertips slipped along the smooth floor, then jerked to a stop on the area of discoloration. It felt rough and warmer in comparison to the rest of the floor. The onset of tears stung her nose. She straightened, exhaled one long breath, then turned back to him.

"Tell me what happened," she said.

"Lady, talk to the police."

"I did."

"You should go."

"You killed my husband. I'm not blaming you. I just want to understand exactly what happened. Tell me, and I'll go."

Andrews sighed. He hitched up his shorts and crossed the room. He stopped at the hallway to the bedrooms. "See, I heard something. I grabbed my gun and came out of my bedroom. I saw your husband standing there. I said something like 'Hey, who the fuck are you?'" He winced. "Sorry."

"Go on." Tonya sat down on the far end of the couch so she could see both the spot and Andrews.

"So I see him raise his gun. And mine, it's already up, you know. Guess it was instinct. I squeezed the trigger. A lot, I guess. Until he fell down."

She imagined her husband falling, tilting, sliding, descending, and wondered what he thought. Had he thought of her in those last seconds? Was it seconds or minutes of life after he fell down? She turned her head away from the thought, closed her eyes against the image of Sam bleeding slowly on the wood floor. When she opened her eyes, she saw Andrews, looking uncomfortable. She blinked back tears.

"So he raised his gun."

Andrews nodded.

"And you were standing right there?"

"No, I was closer to my bedroom."

"Down the hall then?" She walked over to him, pointing down the dark hallway.

"Right."

"What was he doing?"

Andrews cocked his head at her again. "What do you mean?"

"Was he picking up something? Did he have his back to you when you came out of the room, so he had to turn around to see you?"

"No, he just turned his head to look at me."

"So he saw you first?"

"I guess."

"But you were able to fire first."

"Guess I was the faster draw." Andrews began to smile, then remembered whom he was talking to and stopped it.

"I guess so. Would you show me how he was standing when you came out?"

"Look, lady—"

"Call me Tonya."

That seemed to soften him. "I don't think this is going to help you get over your loss."

"I just want to understand." She let a couple tears fall, wiping them away with the backs of her hands.

"Sure."

He came over to the spot near the discoloration, and Tonya went down the hallway.

"I'll be you," she said. He closed his eyes, remembering. First, he turned to face her, then adjusted, angling his left side away from her. He was facing the hallway for the front door, not the bedrooms.

"He had his gun in this hand," Andrews said, making his right hand into a gun, three fingers withdrawn into his palm. His other hand was doing something odd.

"And the left hand? It was just like that?" Tonya said.

Andrews glanced down. His left hand was held up to his side, the fingers of that hand seemed to be cupping his belly. "Yeah, I remember it like that."

Tonya walked slowly down the hall towards Andrews, picturing her husband. Sam, five foot ten, dressed in black, a black bag slung over his back, holding a gun and his stomach. His eyes widened, implored her, his mouth opened when she reached the juncture between the two hallways. She looked at the front door. Then back to Fred Andrews. "How many people did you hear?"

Andrews swallowed. "I saw one guy."

Tonya frowned. "Okay," she said, "what was he after do you think? He didn't have anything on him. I'm wondering what he might have been after."

"You'd know better than me, I think."

"No jewelry, paintings?" They both eyed the green painting.

"The expensive stuff is in the bedroom."

"I see. Well, thank you for your time, Mr. Andrews. Good luck selling the house." She left him standing in his living room.

———•◦•———

Tonya had been a thief. Sam too. They stole things at the request of others. Jewelry, mostly, but cars, boats, and documents too. Sam disliked stealing information. Papers had little tangible value to him. He normally avoided taking on those kinds of jobs. Tonya had no such reservations. He'd been after documents when they met. But she had broken in first and had what he was looking for. She remembered the look on his face when he entered the study. Finding not only the safe open but empty too. He turned around and saw Tonya standing there. He looked her up and down.

"I think you've got something of mine," he said.

She was closer to the door and maybe could've made it, but she saw him shift and realized he'd catch her easily. It was the way he dropped his shoulders and planted his foot. In the short run, she'd be beaten. "So what do you want to do about it?"

"You could give it to me," he said.

She shook her head.

"Or I could take it from you." She stiffened. He frowned and said,

"No. I hate when people try to get cute. Look, they're playing us against each other."

She settled against the nearest wall.

"Let's say I get papers from you but have to hurt you in the process. Then there's evidence. A body, maybe," he said. She glowered at him. He put his hands up. "Okay, maybe there's a little blood, from one of us."

"Gracious of you," she said.

"I try. Now, with the evidence, somebody—your client or mine—could call the police. They try to connect the dots, and then one of us is up to our eyeballs in this."

"And you're dead."

He pointed a thick finger at her. "Yeah, I'm dead, but they're chasing after you."

Tonya frowned. She was in the system, albeit for a minor infraction when she was eighteen. She'd been swept up with a hardheaded boyfriend, fingerprinted, then released. But still, she was in the system.

"I propose a deal," he said.

She listened and agreed. They informed their clients of the other's intentions, split the documents, and delivered half to each client. Neither side was pleased, but they had bigger issues to deal with than Sam and Tonya. The money was nonrefundable as far as Tonya was concerned, and Sam had similar rules, so each got paid. No half-now, half-later bullshit.

Sam appeared outside her apartment off Tropicana Avenue a week later. She'd liked the look of him from the moment they met. She liked his bulk. He brought dinner, not flowers, and for that, she liked him even more. They didn't work for a while, the fallout from the last job still too fresh for new work, so they had time to get to know each other.

Three months later, they worked a job together in Florida, stealing someone's boat. They delivered it and walked away, only to find out later that a body was hidden in it, along with a quarter-million dollars. Tonya hadn't liked the feel of the job, but that revelation was enough for them to decide that it would be their last. They called themselves lucky and then called themselves retired. Sam went to work for a lock and key company; Tonya found work in a bookstore chain. They were married a few months later, his family attended; her mother sent the sheets two weeks later.

According to Sam, their job in Florida was the one time he ever worked with someone other than his brother. He didn't like the uncertainty of depending on others. Nevertheless, it was clear to Tonya that Sam had worked with someone else in the Andrews house.

She requested the autopsy report from the Clark County coroner's office. It would be close to a week before she received it. She thought about Sam over those days of waiting. During the day, she watched TV and tried to remember to eat. Sam would not have approved of her diet of canned peaches and store-brand marshmallows, but it was something. She did not answer the door, though she heard David calling her name. She did not answer her phone—not for her mother, not for her job, and most definitely not for any of the Goodhearts.

———— ·•·————

The autopsy report arrived in five days. Four bullets were found in his body, five bullet wounds were noted. The fifth wound was on Sam's lower-left side, no bullet found. The police report stated that a bullet had been recovered. It had to be pried out of the brick fireplace and was totally useless for identification purposes. The assumption was that it matched the other bullets; thus, it matched Andrews's gun.

Tonya was convinced that Sam was shot before Andrews walked out of his bedroom. He heard a sound, then got out of bed. He heard a fight, maybe. Then a grunt from Sam when he was shot; a silencer was used. Andrews entered the hallway. Sam raised his gun to defend himself, not against Andrews, against someone in the other hallway. Maybe.

Sam knew the truth. So did Fred Andrews.

———•—

Tonya posted flyers on the doors of the Andrewses' neighbors the next day. She'd copied a lawn-service flyer taken off a house near her apartment complex. She'd slung a messenger bag over her shoulder, put her hair up under a hat, and brought a knife, an unadorned switchblade that she wouldn't mind leaving behind in someone, and a little 9-millimeter Smith & Wesson 3913NL, a present from Sam and a gun she could hide easily under one of Sam's hooded sweatshirts. There was a comfort in wearing something of his. Then she parked a few blocks away and canvassed the Andrewses' neighborhood. Now she waited outside the Andrews house until she saw them leave. It was 5:00PM.

She walked around to the next block and found the house that backed against theirs. It was deserted, red eviction/foreclosure stickers in the front window and on the door. She entered the backyard. She climbed the fence and dropped down behind the Andrewses' big tree with the dirt patch in front of it. She left her bag behind and walked up to the back door. The damage from the last break-in still hadn't been repaired, and she slid the door open easily. She stepped in and listened. There was the electric hum from the refrigerator but nothing else. She shut the door behind her and crept down the hallway. First door to the left was a small bedroom. The door to the

•47•

right, a bathroom; the next door on the right was a slightly larger bedroom. The last door was the Andrewses' master bedroom.

Fred had decked the room out, floor to ceiling, in green paisley print wallpaper. Not pretty at all. Tonya thought his wife was just waiting for a good excuse to get rid of this place. A large master bath opened up next to the bedroom. The Roman-style tub was elevated two stairs up from the tiled floor. Double sinks, shower stall, and toilet behind a door. The other quarter of the room was a walk-in closet. Tonya flicked on the light. Shoes in boxes lined the floor under the hanging clothes. Winter clothes were shoved in the back. It was dark back there. The single light was not enough. She turned off the light, nestled herself down in the corner of the closet, and waited for the couple to return.

Her mind wandered in the hours she had to sit there. She remembered the day they found out that Sam was sterile. The panicked look he'd given her. She'd squeezed his hand and asked the questions. They had options: adoption, of course, sperm donors, and, at the very least, a second opinion. Tonya had very much wanted that. Sam rebuffed it all. In the hallway outside of the doctor's office, he leaned back against the wall, shoved his hand in his pockets, and said, "If you were smart, you'd leave me now."

"Guess I'm not," Tonya said, leaning into him. "Besides, who would I leave you for?"

"David."

David had a daughter that he never saw, by choice. It was proof that he could procreate, if not parent.

"I don't want David." Tonya kept her voice level.

Sam had wrapped his arms around her and pulled her closer, whispering "good" into her hair.

She wiped at her face now with the bottom of a wool coat. She didn't like this memory. She didn't like any of the times she had lied to her husband. Minor infractions of purses bought and major ones, like the one told that day. Tonya knew that if she had met David first, she would have never given Sam another look. David was every bit the bad boy. He liked the finer things. Like his suit at the funeral, Armani. He drove a whisper-silent BMW and maintained a condo on the Strip. He charmed and lied. He was an obedient, clean-shaven thug who enforced his father's will on others. And he enjoyed it. He would have been the perfect guy for her to fall for, then be dumped by. She felt guilty for admitting it, even to herself. But she had met Sam first, and by the time she saw David, she was mostly immune to those charms. Sam anchored her. He made Tonya want to be good and walk the straight line. With Sam at her side, she could be a different person. Without him, she could only be what she knew. She knew how to steal, how to lie, and, if necessary, how to hurt those who didn't capitulate to her needs.

She drew her knees up to her chest and put her head down. She was asleep before she even considered that it might be a bad idea.

———•◆•———

Fred Andrews's singing woke her. Tonya winced and lifted her head slowly. His rendition of "Come On, Eileen" might have woken her husband it was so piercing. She checked the time on her cell phone. She'd been there for almost four hours. The couple wobbled into Tonya's line of sight. Andrews was draped over his wife, and she was stumbling under his weight.

"No, come on, Eileen. Come on, Fred. Just make it to the bed," she said.

They disappeared out of view. He sang on. The bed springs squeaked when Fred hit it, and he let out an "oof" in the middle of his chorus.

"Could you have gotten any drunker, Fred?" she said.

"Ah, Janice. Don't be that way. Come here."

"I don't think so, mister," she sang.

"Where you going?"

"I'll be back. Go to bed."

Tonya heard the soft squishing of Janice's shoes on the carpet turn into clacking as she moved away from the bedroom. Tonya listened until the footsteps faded, then she listened for Fred. She heard his belt buckle as he undid it, the zipper as he pulled it down, and the buckle again as it gave a muffled clunk against the floor.

Tonya stretched one leg out in front of her, then the other, rolled her shoulders and her neck. She stood up. She walked to the closet's doorway and peered out. Andrews was sitting on the edge of his bed, his pants around his ankles and his eyes shut. She stepped out into the illuminated bedroom, walked quietly up to the man, and punched him in the face. Her hand hurt immediately. She wondered briefly if she broke his nose. He fell backward holding his face, groaning. She jumped on him, straddling his chest with her knees on his upper arms.

"You lied to me, Fred," she said.

"What's going on?" Fred's eyes darted back and forth. His nose wasn't bleeding much. Tonya was a little disappointed.

"Focus, Fred, right here." She slapped his face. "Remember me?"

"The wife," he said.

"Yes, the wife." She pulled out the knife, flicked its blade open, and laid it against the man's neck. "How many people were here when you shot my husband?"

"I don't know."

She pressed the knife harder against his neck. He sucked in a breath.

"Tell me, Fred, what kind of wife is Janice? Is she the kind of who'd hunt me down for killing her husband? Would she say fuck the police and the justice system and come after me for killing you? Is she that kind of wife?" Tonya grabbed him by the hair and pulled back, pressing the knife against his throat again. She leaned over him, held his gaze.

"I don't know how many were here. At least one other. I saw him run out."

"One?" She pressed harder, and blood flowed in a thin rivulet down onto the bedspread.

"Yes, goddamnit, one. Next day, I got a call. A man said to change my story and say I shot him five times. I wouldn't get in trouble, and I'd get fifteen grand for my cooperation."

"Fred," a voice said.

Tonya leaped off the man, pulled the gun from its holster, and pointed it at Andrews's wife. She had a poker from the fireplace in her hand. Fred tried to stand up, got tangled up in his pants, and fell down between the women.

"You can put it down," Janice said to Tonya. To her husband, she said, "Fred, how could you?"

"That son of a bitch broke into our house."

"So you take money for killing a man?"

"I didn't take money for it."

"Yes, you did. It's what you used for the down payment on the place in Boca, isn't it?"

"Who brought you the money?" Tonya asked.

The couple looked over at her.

"Janice, call the police," Fred said.

"Yes, Janice, call the police so I can tell them what I know. So you can lose the house in Boca and have to stay here in this house."

Janice's eyes widened. She turned on her husband.

"Janice . . ." he said.

"Shut up, Fred." Janice turned back to Tonya. "I am so very sorry for your loss."

"I'm very sorry for my loss, too, Janice. We are both very fucking sorry, now what?" Tonya took a step forward. "You're in your early fifties, right? How many more years does Fred have, do you think? Ten, if you're lucky, with the way he drinks. When the day comes for you to pick out your husband's coffin and decide between champagne or Chantilly-blue-colored silk, you call me, and you tell me how sorry you are for my loss. Then you watch them lower your husband—who drives you crazy when he gets drunk and sings stupid songs from the eighties—into the ground, and you'll come home and realize that's it. Call me then and tell me you are sorry for my loss." Tonya shook, her vision blurred, and she felt herself slipping. But an arm held her up.

Janice Andrews hugged Tonya tight, whispering, "It's okay. It's okay," over and over. A minute passed, then Janice loosened her hold and looked at Tonya. "It's okay to be angry."

Fred had moved away and was pulling up his pants and reaching for the phone next to the bed. Janice let Tonya go and snatched the phone away from her husband.

"Don't you dare. Now tell her who brought you the money."

"Janice," Fred groaned.

"Please . . ." Tonya said. She closed the knife and stuck it back into her pocket. The gun went back in its holster.

"I don't know his name, but he must have been his brother or something. He looked just like your husband."

<hr />

It was twenty minutes to the Goodhearts' house. Back in the eighties, when the house was built, there had been the Goodhearts and no one else but the airport that far out. Now the city surrounded their house on the hill.

Tonya pulled into their circular drive and left the Buick parked behind the five others that clogged it. She didn't ring the doorbell. She walked in and drifted down the hallway toward the voices she heard. Near the back of the house, she found the Goodheart men drinking and laughing. They went silent when they saw her.

Her father-in-law turned around in his chair and grinned at her.

"Goddamn, girl, I didn't think you were ever gonna come around. David and I were just deciding on how we were gonna come after you."

He got up and lunged for her, grabbing her arms and pulling her into his chest, lifting and squeezing at the same time. He smelled of cigars and aftershave. Her father-in-law released her and then held her to his side, his hand gripping her shoulder. "David, look who's here."

David set his glass down and rose from his chair. He smiled weakly.

"Michael, I need to talk to you. Alone," Tonya said.

"Of course, sweetheart. Everybody out."

David was the last to leave. He closed the double doors, his face full of concern.

Michael Goodheart sat down in his leather club chair and told her to sit in the matching one. He put his drink next to an ashtray on the little table between the chairs. "Do you want a drink?"

She realized she did, desperately. She wanted to crawl into a bottle and hide. But that was for later. "No."

"Okay, what are we talking about?" He smiled at her, and in that face, she saw Sam. The same round cheeks; the same eyebrows even. She almost laughed. She'd never taken the time to look at her father-in-law before. There were no pictures. Sam brought with him nothing of his family when he married her, and they'd moved in together. A clean slate, he'd said, just my name to remind me where I came from.

Other questions filtered up, stopping her from saying the real reason she was here. "Why did you and Sam stop talking?"

He pulled a cigar from his pocket. "Eh, his mother. She left us, and he blamed me. I told him that his mother was never happy. She had the boys and spent the next ten years going on and on about wanting to leave Las Vegas. I wasn't leaving. All this sun and what, like three weeks of real cold?" he scoffed. "Finally, she did. Just up and left."

"Then, she died." Sam had told her this bit. She died late at night on a rural road. She drove right into one of those big timber telephone poles.

"Yes, and Sam blamed me for that too. I guess he mentioned that to you."

"He never told me why. Only that she died, and he didn't want to see you."

"Well, Sam was like his mother. He wanted things to be a certain way, and when he couldn't get his way, he sulked. He sulked for twenty years."

"David didn't blame you?"

"No, or if he did, he got over it. I'm his father, that's enough for David. Not for Sam, though." He sighed and lit the cigar he'd been holding. He puffed on it a few times, then blew smoke rings her direction. Each one expanding as it drifted toward her, like ripples in water. Tonya thought the rings formed a bullseye, with her father-in-law for the center target.

"I think you should stay here, with us. David is very concerned about you," he said.

"David killed Sam." She tensed, waiting for his reaction, waiting for the outrage and the anger.

Michael tapped his cigar in the ashtray. "No, that guy Andrews, he shot Sam."

"Yes, he shot him four times. But Sam was shot before Andrews saw him. Someone else was in that house with Sam. It had to be David. Sam wouldn't work with anyone but David or me. He trusted his brother."

"My son is dead. My boy." He coughed. He set his cigar in the ashtray. "What are you going to do?"

"I want to know why Sam is dead."

"Why did you want to take Sam away?"

"What? I didn't want to leave." Tonya was confused. She had said nothing about leaving to Sam. Where would she go? Her mother's too small apartment off Howard Street? Tonya left her life in Chicago behind her. Her life had been here with Sam.

"Sam told David different. Sam was gearing up to leave Vegas. A few more months and he would've been gone. I had to do something."

She felt the weight of the days since Sam's death slide fully onto her. Sam died knowing his brother and his father had betrayed him. "David convinced Sam to do one more job. You set him up. There was nothing in that house except a trigger-happy homeowner."

Michael stood. Tonya backed off a step; she reached for the gun under her sweatshirt. "You all are never faithful," he said. "Nothing makes you happy. Sam was a Goodheart. Now either you're a Goodheart like Sam, or you're not. What's it going to be?"

Michael was on her before she could get the gun out. He grabbed her by the hair, threw her into the chair, and held her there with one hand clamped around her throat. Tonya punched and kicked at him. She drew blood on his arms, but he didn't waver, the pressure just built. She blinked away tears.

"Sam loved you. Don't ever doubt that, sweetheart. We all fall for the wrong ones. David did too. He let her go, though. We found out later she was pregnant, but then she had a girl, and I didn't see the point in chasing after another one of you. Maybe when she's older, she'll find her way to the family."

He used both hands now. Tonya was losing focus. Spots appeared before her, obscuring the tunnel vision. She quit pawing at his arms and tried to get the gun. Her fingers closed over the butt of the gun, and her finger found the trigger hollow. She pulled the gun around blindly. One of his hands left her throat, and she gasped for air. He tried to pull the gun from her hand. She squeezed the trigger. Heard him curse. She blinked away the spots before her eyes, tried to point the gun upwards, and squeezed the trigger again. Then Michael was off her. He was on his knees in front of her. His mouth was open, his lips forming words that didn't come.

Freed of his grip, Tonya took more gulping breaths. She didn't hear David enter the room.

"Tonya, give me the gun." He stood over them, but he didn't look at her. He extended his hand. "Give me the gun and then leave." Tonya wiped at her eyes and rubbed her neck. She used the chair to pull herself up to her feet. She staggered backward, bumping into a lamp. David turned.

"Look, I'm sorry he's dead. You made him happy." David reached for her, and she froze. He embraced her, his smooth cheek cool against her own.

"Your father," she said. Her voice was weak, her throat sore.

"I told Sam if he did one last job, he could score enough money that he wouldn't have to worry. All he wanted to do was make you happy. So he took the job. Dad's plan was to let him take the fall. We figured he'd do a little time and be out in a year or two. So I had to shoot him. But that guy shot him before I even heard him come out."

"It's your fault Sam's dead. You killed him."

"And that made you my responsibility."

She tried to pull away from him, but he held her tighter. "No, David."

"You looked so sad at the funeral. I thought we needed to take care of you now. I thought, hoped, maybe you might see something in me. You could be happy with me." He took the empty gun from her hand and pushed her away. "You should go now. I'll take care of this." He pointed at his father, who was now slumped over. His face pressed against the floor. His mouth had stopped moving. David said, "You won't have to worry."

Sunrise

Great Uncle Wayne was throwing rocks at my window again. I opened the window and had to dodge one. "I'm coming. Can't I get dressed?"

"Bring beer, Etta," he whispered up to me then moved off, a white pillowcase swinging from his good left hand. The man was nearly eighty and up until the Spring he'd been pretty spry, but they'd found cancer again. It was his pancreas and a lung. Now Uncle Wayne walked hunched over and miserable all the time, so I brought the beer.

For the last month, and at least twice a week, he'd come and find me in the middle of the night at my house, or sometimes he'd track me down at my boyfriend's house three blocks over. I was less likely to indulge his desires when my own were put on hold, but still he'd try to get me to drive him to Lake Mead or up Mount Charleston so he could be one of the first to see the sunrise. Tonight, I thought it'd be more of the same. Instead, he insisted we track down Lyle, so we went traipsing across Las Vegas from bar to bar trying to find him.

It was nearly midnight when we found Lyle in a country bar. He was line dancing with a tiny woman with brown hair and big blue eyes. She was just the kind of woman who'd leave him inside two years with half of whatever the last woman left him with. When Lyle saw me, he spun her out and kissed her hand. If he'd had a hat on, he'd have tipped it at her. I rolled my eyes. The song ended as he walked over to me.

"Is she going to be your next ex-wife?"

"I'm just killing time."

"Killing time?"

He tilted his head at me like some lovable dog just waiting for permission to jump on your bed and snuggle up. "Till you decide you want to be with me."

I thought of the kiss we shared the night before and I'd spent the day regretting the act and missing him in equal measure. He grabbed my arm and pulled me toward the door. "Let's not keep Wayne waiting."

"How did you know Wayne is here?"

"Lucky guess?" he said smile firmly in place.

I should've known something was up. Wayne gave him hell for not being at the other six bars we searched. Lyle pulled a shovel and a pickaxe from the trunk his car and tossed it into the bed of my truck then slid in beside Uncle Wayne and said, "Let's go Cousin!" Lyle and I aren't really cousins but fifteen years back his mama married my father's frat brother, known to me as Uncle Cecil, which made us "cousins".

"Where are we going?" I asked once all three of us sat shoulder to shoulder across the bench seat. Uncle Wayne didn't say anything right away. We sat in silence for a minute before I decided it was too damn hot. The A/C wasn't working and my tank top was sticking to my back. The only option was to put down the windows and start driving to find a breeze. I drove ten mile-per-hour loops around the vehicles in the bar's parking lot. I yanked the wheel hard around a turn and we all leaned into it, letting the breeze roll over us.

After the next turn Uncle Wayne said, "I want to go visit my Ellen."

Ellen was Wayne's first wife, the one he'd had five children with and cheated on religiously. That hadn't been together for more than twenty years by the time I was born. He'd left her for the slightly younger Marlene back in '62. More importantly, Aunt Ellen was dead. Lyle and I looked at each other. Lyle's look was all raised eyebrows. What can you do? he seemed to be saying. I dutifully turned the truck onto Charleston Boulevard and toward the I-15 on-ramp.

I glanced down and saw the pillowcase between Uncle Wayne's feet. In it was the six-pack of beer I'd promised but he had something else in there too. Every now and again it would clink against the cans.

"What all is in that pillowcase, other than the beer?"

"None of your business." Uncle Wayne kept looking straight ahead.

I sighed. "Does Marlene know where you are?"

"She's asleep. Pay attention to your driving, Etta." He grumbled about women drivers and Lyle snorted.

I shook my head but kept my eyes on the asphalt running under the headlights. "I can drive and talk, Uncle Wayne. Tell me what's going on."

"I just want to see Ellen," he said and wouldn't say another word.

When great Aunt Ellen passed a month ago, I had her cremated as was her wish and the family took her ashes out to the desert. We took her to the place where my dad and uncles would take all the kids out to shoot cans and ride our BMX's in actual dirt. We'd come home filthy and our mothers hated it, but Aunt Ellen never did. She loved to hear the stories of scorpions and snakes and spiders seen and of coyotes heard. This was where we took her ashes and spread them under a flowering cactus where we assumed some divine dust devil would eventually come and scatter her. There was a nearby rock we marked with her initials and a little seven-inch cross Uncle Wayne erected in her memory, much to the disapproval of Marlene. She went so far as to call the Bureau of Land Management to let them know what had been done on their property, but the person at the other end of the line was less than helpful.

Uncle Wayne was not himself these days. He'd gone quiet and when forced to talk, his words were sharp. He had no stories to tell and no desire to play games with younger nieces and nephews. While most of the family had decided to be a little kinder to him and ignore his moods, Marlene took the change in his behavior personally. In the three weeks since the funeral she had cursed and seethed over her husband's display of mourning. Just last night at dinner as we began to eat, she looked at him and said, "You never even loved her. I don't understand why you're so down in the mouth over her now." The sounds of dinner abruptly stopped, and we all looked at each other, at Marlene, then Uncle Wayne.

"I loved her," Uncle Wayne said quietly.

She dropped the ladle in the mash potatoes. "No, you didn't. You told me so."

"I lied, Marlene. I wanted to have you and you wanted to hear I didn't love her, so I told you a lie." Uncle Wayne gestured at the bowl of mash potatoes with his fork and hand as if he could coax it down the table.

Aunt Marlene pushed back from the table and muttered, "If you love her so much then go be with her." She spent the rest of the night shut up in her bedroom while we finished the Sunday dinner we had come for.

———•◦•———

I checked my mirrors then veered off the road, my headlights sweeping the desert as I looked for the familiar landmarks that come and go out here. One year, it was a burned-out car. Another, it was a broke down desk and a gutted couch, but mainly I drove toward a particular rocky outcrop. As we neared it, I stopped the truck and we got out to continue by foot. Lyle pulled the shovel out of the truck bed and I gave him the keys to my toolbox to get the big flashlight. There was a moon out, but it wasn't enough to see our way safely in the desert.

I turned on the flashlight and led the way with its yellowish beam. The light rolled over rocks and making small night animals run from us and shards of glass sparkle like stars. Lyle walked with Uncle Wayne keeping him close. Uncle Wayne walked with both hands strangling the top of the pillowcase. He wouldn't let either of us carry it for him. Finally, I caught the dark figure of the cactus in the flashlight's beam. It's one branch angled up like a crossing guard's arm signaling us to stop. There was gash in the cactus's side now and its flower was gone. I swept the light across the ground. The cross was gone too but the rock was still there. I breathed easier seeing it. Uncle Wayne set the pillowcase next to the rock and stepped into the circle of light and stood reverent in it, his face turned to the night sky. I looked up too. The stars were pinpricks of white light. I looked back toward home and saw our city glowing against the blue-black sky. It was cooler out here away from all the asphalt and concrete. Lyle's hand settled on my shoulder and I leaned into him a little enjoying his solidity and warmth.

"What is he doing?" I said quietly. "Why are we out here, Lyle?"

"He asked me to bring a shovel. I didn't have the heart to tell him no. I figured you would," he said, laughing a little.

Uncle Wayne, apparently done with his reverie, walked over to the rock and picked up the pillowcase. "Here's the deal. I'm supposed to start chemotherapy on Thursday but I'm going to die. There's no avoiding that. I want to go my way. I'm done being poked and prodded by everyone. Lyle, I need you to dig me a hole and I'm going to lie in it and at sunrise I'm going kill myself." From the bag he pulled a gun and held it in the light.

My body went hot then cold. "I don't think so, Wayne Smith." I stepped toward him, but Lyle pulled me back before I did something stupid like hit Uncle Wayne over the head and drag him back to Marlene and the relative safety of our family.

Uncle Wayne walked over and grasped my shaking hand with the one not holding the gun. "Sweetheart, I have lived a long life and screwed up most of it. I am so grateful to have had you in my life. But goddamn, I'm tired and I miss Ellen. I might not get to see her on the other side, but I'd like to think if there was any place she might look down at, it would be here where you kids laughed and played. Maybe she'll wave at me. I don't know."

"But you left her," Lyle said.

He sighed and dropped my hand. "It was foolishness. There I was in the Army, young and black, fit and fine. I'd say, Hello, ma'am, and women would fall out at my feet. I didn't even try to stop myself. Then I met Marlene. She was a USO dancer and I thought I had found the zing of zings. I got back from Vietnam and left Ellen. I thought Ellen would miss me, but she never acted like she did. I married Marlene to show Ellen I didn't need her either. I was wrong but Ellen wouldn't let me come back."

"You tried to come back?" I said. I'd heard about his belief in the zing of zings before but in all my thirty years I'd never heard this story.

"Of course. She was the love of my life." Uncle Wayne bowed his head. I put down the flashlight and hugged him. Lyle dropped the shovel and wrapped his long arms around us both until Uncle

Wayne pushed himself free of our love and pity and pointed at a spot on the ground near the cactus. "It doesn't have to be deep, Lyle."

Lyle began to dig first with the shovel then with the pickaxe. The hard-packed earth didn't want to be disturbed. With every shovelful Lyle moved, he looked at me like I had to be the one to fix this, but Uncle Wayne had worked it all out. Lyle would leave his phone with him and if Uncle Wayne changed his mind, he'd call. If not, come sunrise, we were to drive back here, cover him with dirt and etch his initials into the rock next to Aunt Ellen's.

Lyle hit a large rock and swore. He stopped and wiped his forehead with the bottom of his shirt. "Uncle Wayne, maybe there's another way. Maybe we go home and see what the doctors say?"

"It's all right, son. I got what I need here." Wayne waved the gun at him.

"Uncle Wayne, please." I took his empty hand in mine, but he would not look at me.

"Y'all go on now. Come back later," he said. Lyle took me by the arm for the second time that night and pulled me back to the truck.

I kept thinking Aunt Ellen would understand his choice but at the same time I knew she would hate this. Wasting life was not something she did. Mostly, she spent the bulk of her years working a job and half to keep the house in the decent school district. I went to see her once after a particularly bad high school break up—he played center on the Rams basketball team and the girl he left me for was head cheerleader. It was so clichéd it burned me up even then. Aunt Ellen took me into her bedroom and sat me down on her silk duvet and brushed my hair out while I sobbed fourteen-year-old girl tears. Then she said as she re-braided my hair, "People do what they want. You can't stop them anymore than they can stop you. It's the lucky few who can look back without regret." I took this to mean my basketball player would come back to me. He didn't. I got over him, with a football player.

— •●• —

We had to drive almost all the way to the city of Jean to find a turn-around. Before the turn off for the city we found a long-gone store, its windows boarded up. On the property's little piece of decaying asphalt, we waited with the windows down and watched the clock on my dashboard tick the time away. After a bit we took turns playing a blackjack game on my phone and smoking Lyle's Pall Malls.

I thought of Uncle Wayne alone in the dark with just his memories and that cactus. Yes, he was old. Yes, he may well be dying but should this be his end? Even if it was what he wanted? I could imagine my father's face when he found out his uncle was gone. Grandpa had been dead for years and my father had looked to Wayne as a replacement during the hard times life can thrust upon you. Like the time I brought home a college senior to take me to my high school prom. I wasn't sure what Marlene would do. Probably sell the house and move back Atlanta where her people were from.

The simple truth was, if not for me driving him way out here to the end of his line, he might have gone back to bed and woke up next to Marlene in the morning and thought, good enough. But was "good enough" what I wanted to wake up thinking every day. It wasn't. Hell, I had a boyfriend who, if I would've so much as left a bra at his place, would've asked me to marry him. I never left anything behind. I didn't want to give the impression I wanted to stay. Besides, I could clearly see the road my boyfriend and I were on and it wasn't meant for fast driving and wouldn't end at happily ever after. No, that road was flat, boring and without a twisty turn in sight.

I wanted to do better than that. I wanted zing in my life. Unfortunately, the only zing I had in my life currently was Lyle.

The night before, after Marlene's blowup, Lyle and I finished eating and started on the dinner dishes while our parents and the older folk sat about, talking weather and making meaningful faces at each other about Marlene and Uncle Wayne. After the kitchen was cleaned, we went outside with our beers. It was June and in the evenings the heat was bad but not completely unbearable yet. Out on the patio, Marlene kept a little oasis of plants and flowers alive with a rigged-up misting system so the air was sweet and few degrees cooler than the rest of the world. I leaned back against a post that held up the awning over our heads. Lyle sat back on rocking bench and gave himself a push.

The windows in the dining room were open and we could hear the conversation clearly. I closed my eyes and sipped my beer, loving the feel of night on my bare legs. I didn't realize Lyle had stopped swinging until the pads of his fingers brushed my knee. I could've stopped him there. I could have moved away. But the zing and crackle that zipped through me at his touch pushed away all rational thought. We were moving towards each before I even processed the decision. We stopped after a few minutes 'cause if we could hear them, they could certainly hear us, but it was enough. We hadn't seen each other in the 27 hours since and now, sitting next to him, watching him take a long pull off his cigarette it was all I could do not to slide across the old bench seat and encourage him to pick up where we'd left off the night before.

Instead of acting on that impulse, I watched the way his lips moved around the end of the cigarette and the flex of his strong jaw. When he exhaled and I had to look away. His hand found mine in the dark.

"She filed for divorce, you know." He meant his wife, Janelle.

"Yay for you."

"Etta."

"What? I'd be more impressed if you'd done the leaving or the divorcing. Janelle was not nice to your children." Lyle had twins—perfect little miniature redhead copies of him. Their mother took off to find work in North Dakota and never came back. A year later Lyle found Janelle, his second wife, when she was singing karaoke in a bar he liked to frequent.

"Janelle likes the kids and they like her."

I pulled my hand away and tossed my phone down. It bounced off the seat between us and tumbled into the wheel well by his feet. "The last time she brought the kids to the local pool, she was so busy gossiping about this, that, and the other, she wouldn't have known if Little Lyle was drowning or swimming. And she filled Belle's head with so many 'Cosmo-rules-for-living' that Belle wouldn't get in the water. When I asked her why, she said because the swimsuit was 'for looks, not swimming.'"

He sighed and looked away.

"I like my life. I don't want to be anyone's step-mama. Find some other girl."

"You want to grow old alone?"

I thought of Uncle Wayne and Aunt Ellen. "Being alone is better than growing old with the wrong person."

Lyle didn't have anything to say after that.

———— ••• ————

By 5AM, we'd stopped playing blackjack and were just smoking, passing a cigarette back and forth to preserve our dwindling supply. My phone lay between us with a 5% charge.

"Shit," Lyle said.

The first streaks of morning could be seen. I swallowed hard trying not to cry. This was what he wanted, I told myself, blinking back tears.

"Do you think he really did it?" Lyle's voice was low and edged with something. Fear, I supposed.

"Of course, he did," I said, my voice meaner than I intended. I turned on the ignition and pulled off our asphalt oasis onto the road headed back to Las Vegas. Lyle tried to find a radio station. Every song that played made his shoulders hunch up.

"Leave it," I said. He turned his head away, but I could still hear the little gasps he gave up as he tried and failed to keep from crying.

There were more cars out, people driving in from California or maybe home from the Primm casinos. They honked as I slowed the truck and took it out onto the gravel middle. I let my right hand leave the wheel and my fingers began to drum idly on the leather seat. Lyle reached over and grabbed my hand again, threading his fingers between mine and I let him. We turned onto the road leading away from the city and back to Uncle Wayne, the night fading on one side of us and the new day rising on the other.

Maybe I should've said something to ease Lyle's fears. Hell, it was possible we'd careen through the desert, a plume of dirt kicked up behind us, and arrive just in time to sit next to Uncle Wayne, crack a beer, and watch the sun burn the last bit of night from the sky. The thought that he might still be there made my vision go blurry. I squeezed Lyle's hand. We turned off the highway and I drove fast through the desert hoping to get to Uncle Wayne before the sun did.

Hello, My Name Is Denise

"**I** saw God once."

A man in a blue trucker hat laughed. It cut through the silence of the small building. He and the man next to him sat in the back row wearing matching Carhartt jackets. Blue Hat chuckled again, nudging the other, who shook his head. The green brim of his trucker hat dipped down as if he was trying to hide. Denise guessed Blue Hat was Green Hat's support system. They were all supposed to bring someone, but Denise's grandmother was working the polls that night. The only other person she'd wanted there was Dumont, and he was too far away to drop in. Denise saw the disbelief on Blue Hat's face. It was on the faces of many in the audience, they too had seen God and Santa Claus and the Easter bunny, all while in their own personal stupors.

"I know what you're thinking," Denise continued. "It wasn't that way, and it wasn't in some weird near-death experience with me floating over an operating table but in the alley behind Grouper's Tavern in Las Vegas. Sure, I was drunk, but not good drunk. Good drunk is when I can't remember what happened after the last shot.

I remember that night and how I ended up in that alley, face down and bleeding at God's feet."

Denise looked up at the drop ceiling, at the stained acoustic tiles. The building was used mostly for Sunday Bible classes and daycare. She stood on a low stage, behind a podium that hid most of her small frame. Participants were encouraged not to use the podium.

You are among friends. You have nothing to hide, the counselor had told her. Denise agreed she didn't have anything to hide, but she thought a little stationary support couldn't hurt. She pieced together a bigger smile, her cashier smile, the one that made her words bouncy and bubbly. The smile that made customers comment on how nice she was as she bagged their groceries and sent them on their way.

"You see, my guy and me, his name was Wardell, fine ass, quick-trigger temper when intoxicated. Intoxicated, that's the counselor's word, not mine. We were celebrating my new job, my second in as many months, and my buying a new car. My first new car. It was a sturdy, little, blue Ford Focus. Wardell twirled the keys to it on his finger as we made our grand entrance into Grouper's. He immediately bought the whole bar a round of shots. A cheer went up, and men raised glasses to him in thanks. Now nobody really cared for Wardell, they thought he was too young to swagger the way he did. Too young for me, too. He was nearly six years younger. However, if somebody was buying them drinks, who were they to say no? Yeah, it was my money Wardell was spending, he'd been in between jobs for most of our relationship, but I let him. When Wardell was happy, I was too."

Denise was interrupted by the squall of a metal door opening at the back of the room. Dumont was there, all long limbs and dressed in slacks, a crisp white shirt, and a tie, of all things, like she was graduating from college or something instead of receiving her thirty-day chip. He was dressed up as if he thought she was special when she knew she wasn't. Or, at least, not special enough. He smiled at her, then found a chair in the back row with the men in trucker hats.

She bit her lip, wiped her hands on her jeans, and tugged at her sweater. The sticker with her name on it crackled. She smoothed it back into place. She looked out at the people sitting clustered together in the center of rows of metal folding chairs. It was only a dozen people, but she could feel their varying degrees of impatience. Tonight, in front of these people, some she knew on sight, if not by name, others she didn't know at all, Denise was telling the truth.

"Wardell swung me up onto a stool. I sat facing out into the bar, watching the shots go round. I had mine, slammed the little glass down onto the bar with the rest of them, and we all enjoyed the burn. I was a little tired, but I put on my best smile. It was easy with Wardell next to me, one hand on my thigh, the other on his beer, like he did when we were at his place or mine. Like usual, his hand crept up my thigh, sneaking under the hem of my skirt where his fingers slipped up and down while he talked hockey with his buddy, Dumont. In high school, they'd played football together, both of them linebackers. Long after they'd given up on their athletic dreams, they still hung out. Dumont raised his beer to me. I grinned back. He was always good to be around. He always had a calming effect on Wardell. Whenever Wardell said we were going out, I always hoped Dumont would join us.

"Another round of shots was ordered. I had another shot directly after that, then I ordered a Corona, so I was early drunk, only leaning a little. I listened to the hum of the bar, to the music that leaked from the jukebox, and to the clink of glasses on tabletops. It was a good night so far. I leaned closer to Wardell and listened to him and Dumont talking about the Olympics and how Wardell thought there was something about those Mary-Lous. Him going on and on about the Mary-Lous, saying that there was hardly nothing to them but when they got up on the beam and did that flip—you know the one where the girl lands, straddling the beam?—and how he couldn't help but imagine her doing that flip onto him in a bedroom setting.

"Now, Dumont is a nice guy, with a sweet, round face and big brown eyes. I've never known him to say an unkind word to anyone, so of course he laughed, but not in that big robust way he normally laughed. His laugh has been known to shake doors and windows in their frames. Not that Wardell noticed. He was caught up in his vision of that gymnast. Then he started talking about another girl, one who was obviously not even sixteen yet, and I said as much kind of under my breath.

"I didn't think he heard me. The hand under my skirt was still there, trying to slip ever northward, his fingers dug in deep between my crossed thighs. I realized a little late that people in the bar were looking at me funny. Old men half-grinning, waiting for a little flash of panty to go with their free drink, and one older woman, one who'd prettied herself up and squeezed into a black lacy tube top, was giving me the side eye. I tried to get Wardell to quit it without actually having to say anything. I squirmed and tried to keep my beer from spilling while he talked on, his head turned away from me. I tried to gently shove his hand down with my right hand and keep my stool from swiveling too much. Then my beer spilled onto my skirt and down his arm. He yelled and tried to yank his hand away, but it being August at the time, it was just this side of too warm in the bar. His hand stuck to me the way I used to stick my grandma's plastic-covered couches during my summer vacations. Wardell ended up pulling me half-off my stool before his hand finally ripped free of my tacky thigh. The beer I was holding was still near full; once I lost my grip on the bottle, it landed on his thigh and fell over, neck down, spreading its ice-cold essence liberally across his crotch.

"At this point, y'all can be sure that Wardell was done being happy for the night."

A couple of people shifted in their metal seats, but their eyes never left Denise's face. One or two smiled up at her. Denise smiled back. Denise looked right at Dumont when she said "Sweet-face Dumont ran interference for me. I scooted off to the back of the bar, where the back door was kept open for the smokers since Vegas went smokeless and where the bathrooms were. Before I went into the ladies' room, I looked back and saw the bartender toss a towel Wardell's way. He pressed at his crotch with it, trying to sop up some of the mess. I was truly hoping he wouldn't come back to where I was. Dumont was loud talking to him, trying to calm him down, and Wardell just cussed on and on while everyone around him laughed good-naturedly.

"In the bathroom, I tried to salvage my work skirt, dabbing at the dark spots as best as I could with the completely nonabsorbent brown paper towels, you know the ones supplied in most low-caliber establishments all over these United States of ours? Sure, Wardell was pissed and maybe uncomfortable, but he was wearing the black jeans I'd bought him the week before, so he'd be fine in the bar. I was in my work clothes. My skirt was dry clean only. After the rounds of drinks bought and coming up with the down payment on the car, I knew I'd barely have enough to make it to my next payday, so paying to have my clothes dry cleaned wasn't an option that week.

"I kept at my skirt, though. Praying it wouldn't look so bad, that maybe I could get another wearing out of it. That's when I realized I was trying to dry new spots. In the mirror over the bathroom's sinks, I saw tears were pouring down my cheeks and splattering onto my blouse and skirt. Now I wasn't wailing or about to have a real my-heart's-in-it crying jag. The tears just fell. I guessed three hours spent car hunting and haggling over prices had worn me out. I should have let Wardell party without me.

"I suppose I stayed out with him because of the car. I wasn't worried about Wardell cheating on me, because I knew at his worst he'd only hook up with a girl long enough to get her to give him a blow job in a dark corner somewhere. Then he'd come home to me, all excited and eager and not caring a bit that I'd been sleeping. He'd fuck my dead body, I think, then complain about my lack of passion. No, it was my new car with its new car smell and the courtesy paper still on the floorboards so the carpet wouldn't get dirty. My new car that I hadn't gotten to drive once since I signed the paperwork for it. All I had gotten was the test drive. After that, I'd let Wardell have his way. He wanted to drive, so he drove."

Denise paused here and took a sip of water from the plastic cup on the podium. She glanced at where Dumont sat hunched over with his hands between his knees as if bracing for the blow he knew was coming. Denise let go of her smile.

"I was being silly, I told myself. I shook my head at my reflection in that mirror, patted at my face with those useless paper towels, fixed my hair, and assembled the pieces of a smile onto my face before I pulled open the bathroom door. The jukebox was playing, but through the Grouper's unfortunate speakers, all you could hear was tinny bassline. I looked out into the bar. Dumont was at the jukebox with his back to me. The bartender was leaning way over the bar to whisper into some blonde girl's ear. Wardell's narrow-eyed face, tinged red under the deep-brown skin, leaped into focus as he grabbed me by the neck.

"He yanked me clear out of one shoe. He switched his grip to grab me by my hair and half dragged, half pushed me out the back door. All the while, I was gasping and stumbling, trying to keep up. In the alley, there was nothing but empty beer boxes stacked and the nasty-smelling dumpster, all just barely lit up by the back door's overhead light. Wardell spun me around. I blinked, trying to focus, feeling the full effect of the shots and the beer in my system. I closed my eyes again. Before I could open them, pain thumped through my head like a thunderclap. Heat swarmed into my ear. He hit me again, probably because I was still on my feet, and he broke my nose with that hit."

Denise touched her nose and grimaced, remembering the pain, that white-hot lightning that shot through her face and made her knees go wobbly. Someone grunted in the front row, a man Denise had seen a few times. His cheeks and nose still held the too-bright redness from a long history of alcohol. He nodded at her, urging her on.

"I hit the ground. He leaned over me and said, real quiet like, 'Did I ask your opinion on the age of that girl? No, I did not. You're old, Denise. Old and used. I think I need me a new model.' Then he kicked me. Now, I'm sure he was aiming for my stomach, but he'd had a fair amount to drink himself, and he lost his balance a little, so his kick landed with less force and on my leg. Not that it didn't hurt. That muscle rolled itself up tight as hell almost immediately. I was whimpering and holding my leg and nose. I heard Wardell cuss and saw his foot rise again, but then he just left me there. I didn't get up. I thought someone would come for me. Someone had to see him drag me out. I just stayed there and cried until I passed out.

"When I woke up, I thought I'd heard my name. I felt the ground under my cheek—a rock was jabbing me there—and I opened my eyes a little, fully expecting to see Wardell's brown, steel-toe boots scuffed and tapping impatiently near my head. He'd either be wait-ing to apologize or to begin round two. The light was brighter than I remembered and at first, I didn't see anything but the empty beer boxes next to the dumpster. For just a second, I closed my eyes, then reopened them and saw a dark, backlit figure. Figuring it was Wardell, I tried to curl up real tight, like they tell you to do when confronted with a bear on your camping trip. But then this voice floated down to me, real soft and low, and said my name like it's never been said before or since. So of course I looked up again, because this voice could not belong to Wardell. In my head, though, I was thinking, Please don't let this be the nightmare where the nice guy turns into Wardell accusing me of cheating again.

"I said, 'Yes?' but it was slurred to my own ears. I coughed and spat blood, then felt the full-on body ache hit me.

"When I was done spasming and crying, I looked around again and there He stood. Not in the weak-ass, low-wattage light from Grouper's dollar-store light bulbs but in a pure white light that lit him up and made his brown hair shine and glinted off his handlebar mustache."

A woman laughed. Next to her, a man leaned in close to her and whispered low and furious into her ear. Her face fell. She looked away from Denise. The man crossed his arms over his chest and focused his attention back on Denise. Denise understood how she must sound to that woman and felt the need to acknowledge her.

She put her hands up and said, "I know how this must sound, but it was one of those Wyatt-Earp-in-the-O.K.-Corral-type mustaches, and behind that was the kindest face I've ever seen. I swear to you, I stopped hurting in that first moment. My nose didn't throb in his presence. The ground wasn't as hard any longer but soft like the grass you only remember in dreams about your childhood."

Denise looked out across the room to Dumont, who watched her steadily. She wondered what he saw. If he only saw the old Denise. The one who was always a little too drunk to walk properly. The one who rolled over for Wardell at the snap of his fingers. That Denise, she was ashamed of her. She wanted Dumont to know that she had changed. She was doing the hard work of living all by herself. Well, for the most part anyway. She didn't make enough to have a place by herself, but she was working on it. The next words Denise said were for Dumont, and she made sure he was listening when she continued her story.

"'What are you doing down there?' the man said. And if that wasn't the question of all questions! What was I doing down there, other than crying and bleeding? I shrugged, which did hurt a little. 'You gotta help yourself, Denise.' Then I heard my grandma, loud and clear in my head, say 'God helps those who help themselves,' and I remembered something. It was this:

"My grandma spent nearly the whole of her marriage taking care of my grandpa. A year after my mom was born, Grandpa fell at a construction site, hitting his head. He never spoke again after that day, or kissed my grandma or my mom, or ever managed to wipe his own ass again, but Grandma never wavered in her devotion to him. You gotta imagine my grandma, no taller than me, and she was skinny, frail looking. She had the look of always being tired, I mean, even her skin looked tired. But long after my mom escaped that life, Grandma took care of that man alone. Eventually, though, the guilt caught up with my mom in San Diego, and she sent me to do her penance.

"For three summers, I gave up the ocean and balmy summer days to sweat it out in the heat and humidity of Chicago while I helped my grandma take care of her husband. I fed him and wiped his mouth when she was busy selling bottles of RC Cola and red popsicles for a quarter each out her back door to the local kids. While she gave him a bath, I mopped and waxed her kitchen floor. For all the work, though, I enjoyed it at her place. In San Diego, I'd spent days on end fending for myself while my mom would be out enjoying her time with some man or sleeping off her alcohol stupor in the drunk tank. But at Grandma's, after Grandpa was in bed, we'd sit out on the back porch and watch the fireflies go by. It was a night like that when I asked Grandma why she didn't put Grandpa in a home.

"She was sitting in the straight-backed kitchen chair with a bottle of RC in her hand. Without looking at me, she said, 'That's my husband you're talking about. Be careful.' I was twelve then. I knew I crossed some line, but I told her I was only saying what my mama said. Grandma made a face. I thought she was angry, but now I realize she was tired, and she said, 'God helps those who help themselves.'

"Over the years, I came to think she meant she was obligated to take care of her husband; that her life was traded for his. I didn't want that for me. The one thing my mama taught me was to go after the good times, because you never knew when they were gonna end. So I tried to live my life like that. But lying there in that alley, bleeding at the feet of the Almighty, I realized that my mama, for all of her good times, had nothing to show for it, and those men she had those good times with always left her. I decided there in that alley that helping yourself can mean a lot of different things, and that night it meant that Wardell wasn't good for me, but unless I gave him up I'd never be free of him, nobody could intervene on my behalf. Dumont couldn't distract Wardell long enough for me to ever truly escape him. I had to do it. So I said, 'Okay, but could I ask for a hand up off the ground?' But in the time it took me to remember my grandmother's words, He was gone.

"Then I got up real slow on my own. My face felt twice its normal size. My nose felt big, sore, and it was throbbing something mighty. I stood, finally, and looked both directions down the alleyway, but there was no one to see, only the red from the streetlight or from a car's taillights. I limped back into the bar and found it near empty. The bartender and the same blonde were cozied up at the far end of the counter. I could see my purse near the cash register. I hobbled over; the bartender brought it to me. He offered to call an ambulance, but I just asked for a cab. Dumont came out from one of the corner booths, took one look at me, and told me he was taking me home. I let him. It's not like I had money for a cab after all. Nobody mentioned Wardell. I didn't ask about him. I figured he had my car. I thought maybe I'd report it stolen after I had some sleep and aspirin. Overall, I felt good leaving that bar without Wardell.

"Dumont eventually talked me into going to the ER. They did what they could for my nose. I'm lucky. It could be much worse than having this little bump on my nose. So it leans to the left; I could still be in that alley.

"I know y'all are thinking that I didn't meet God in the alley. Maybe you're right. All I saw was a dark figure who told me to get up off the ground on my own. Hardly a biblical meeting, right? Can y'all see Charleston Heston talking about the Ten Commandments, then saying 'Hey, did you hear the one about the drunk chick behind that bar in Vegas?'" There was laughter. "Getting here wasn't easy. I don't have to tell y'all that. But here I am."

She didn't say all she thought. She didn't say how much she missed drinking, nearly everyone in her audience knew that loss. For a long time, drinking and Wardell went in hand in hand, one never one without the other. The Wardell-shaped hole in her life was constant and unfillable, she thought.

No one clapped for her. Denise stepped off the stage, her eyes on Dumont in the back row. She shook hands with a few people. Then everyone else made their slow, shuffling way towards the refreshment table on one side of the room. Denise weaved between the empty chairs to sit next to Dumont. His head was down, cradled in his hands. Denise sat close enough to feel the warmth of his body.

"You couldn't save me that night, Dumont. I was trying to tell you that."

He nodded. "You sounded real good up there."

"Thanks for coming. You didn't need to. You could've just called me back."

He shrugged. "Wasn't nothing. I've got people out this way. I'm staying with a cousin." He lifted his head from his hands and looked her over. "And you called. It was good to hear your voice. It's better seeing you, though."

She felt herself blush.

"Maybe you'll let me take you out?" Dumont asked.

"I'm not like I was before. I'm not her anymore." Denise was more on her own after ten years living in Vegas. She didn't want a new man to lead her through life again.

"Then I need to get to know this Denise."

She didn't know how to say that she was afraid Wardell was the one she was meant to be with. How, for all his flaws, he'd made her feel alive. That every day she found herself looking in every bar window, checking out every man in slouching jeans and a white tank top. Every tattooed bicep made her remember Wardell and pulled at her heart. Every man who said "hello" was almost Wardell.

Denise nodded and held out her hand. Dumont shook his head, but he took her small hand in his. They shook hands like strangers.

"I'm Dumont," he said.

She smiled up at him. "Hello, my name is Denise."

On Monday Nights We Danced in the Park

Daddy died the same week my divorce came through.

He died in the kitchen while eating toast over the sink, probably contemplating the Bears' chances at another Super Bowl, letting the crumbs tumble over his beard and into the chrome basin. When the heart attack struck, it yanked him from where he stood and hurled him face down onto my mother's tile floor. Hearing his cup shatter, Mom went running, thinking he'd found her Christmas present hiding place among the pots and pans below the counter. Though I never told her, he and I had found it years ago. After the holidays, she never bothered to hide presents again.

Mom had been in the laundry room folding towels while talking on the phone with some local cousin about the Happy Divorcée party she was planning for me. Party planning was her new obsession. Already she'd planned three events that year: her own wedding anniversary, held at the private golf club Daddy belonged to; my dog Bardot's first birthday, thrown at a park with a dozen neighborhood dogs and their owners' families, which ended when the birthday girl chewed through the cord to the speakers' set-up for the DJ and nearly electrocuted herself; my own birthday party, which was held at a bowling alley where we wore matching bowling shirts and had a bowling-pin-shaped cake. I was the one who planned Daddy's funeral. Her only input was the number for a caterer. She wasn't interested in washing dishes for hours like she did at Thanksgiving.

I was in my living room, hungover and heartsick, crying while separating DVDs into His and Hers. Bardot watched from her perch on the couch, likely wondering when her other person was coming back. Since Sam left, instead of turning in a circle and flopping down for sleep at night, Bardot would sniff Sam's side of the bed, then go to the front door, sniff it, and return to look at me. This she did three times before finally flopping down in the doorway of the bedroom, as if positioning herself there guaranteed her not missing him when he returned. How do you explain to a dog that its favorite person wasn't coming back? How do you explain to anyone?

———•———

At the funeral, Mom channeled Eartha Kitt and Jackie Kennedy, wearing big sunglasses, a black sheath, and leopard-print high heels. I wore a matching dress but plain-Jane flats that weren't nearly up to the job of keeping my toes warm. At the gravesite, all of us were swathed in scarves and thick coats to fend off Chicago's winter cold. I didn't watch the coffin descend into the ground. I watched my mother's mouth fold into a small, tight frown that lingered on for months.

The extended family showed up at the house with wide smiles and homemade food: macaroni, sweet potato pie, and apple cobbler. Then they settled into gossiping about this cousin and that aunt's bad behavior. Some of the men, tall men like my father, their skin the same warm, deep brown as his, gathered in the backyard to smoke and drink away from the womenfolk. I tried to sit with them, a little desperate to feel some of Daddy's energy from a relation of his. One of them spotted me and said, "Hey there, little one. How you doing? How's your mother?" He drank deep from a can of beer, emptying it, and then tapped the ash from his cigar into the can. I caught some uncomfortable shifting among the menfolk.

I reported that my mother was fine. Three men guffawed. Another coughed into his fist; all their exhaled breaths combined to create a haze that hovered over our heads.

He smiled at me and winked. "That she is, little one. You tell your mother that when she's ready, she should give me a call."

I went back into the house.

In the living room, I sat in Daddy's wingback chair and let the smell of his sandalwood-scented pomade and Pall Mall cigarettes overwhelm me. Mom never let him smoke in the house, but the smoke attached itself to everything and every place Daddy frequented, mostly the downstairs bathroom and his favorite chair. I missed the smell of him. I missed our weekly poker game, where he regularly made twenty dollars off me and, when my back was turned, put sixty in my wallet. I missed him. And in missing him, I found myself missing my ex-husband so acutely I had to struggle to breathe.

Sam hadn't come. The night before the funeral, he called from his new apartment in San Francisco. "I'm sorry I can't be there, Marissa."

"It's okay." It wasn't, and he knew it wasn't, but we weren't family anymore, so I couldn't be angry with him. Still, I was.

"Your dad was a great guy." Sam's voice broke. That night, I couldn't bear to hear him cry when I was still surrounded by the ruins of our marriage.

"I'll let you go," I said.

"Sure," he said, "you're good at that."

"You moved out."

"You didn't even try to stop me."

"Sam, was I supposed to write you love letters? Serenade you with a boom box?"

"That would've been something," he sighed. "Look, this isn't why I called. I loved your father. I still care about you, so if you want to talk to me, you can."

I hung up on him.

Our marriage, the whole two years of it, was nothing special, and the end was nothing explosive. We each wanted things the other couldn't give, not to mention that we fought over everything: He left the toilet paper holder empty. I drank out of the orange juice carton. He ate the last of something and left the empty container on the counter. I refused to vacuum. Oh, and another little thing: Sam wanted us to have a baby, like now. I wanted more time. Time he didn't want to give.

Sitting in my parents' living room thinking about Daddy and Sam, tears welled up but didn't fall. I stood to leave and in doing so, caught the attention of the women in the room. The oldest women, four ladies who might be cousins twice removed or in-laws of one sort or another, rallied and circled around me, all clucking tongues and mournful faces, saying, Poor honey, lost your husband and your father in the same week.

"It's terrible," said one.

"Do you think your husband will come back?" asked another.

I stammered that he hadn't left me. That we decided to end it. It was amicable, our divorce. Four pairs of eyes met. Four sets of eyebrows rose knowingly.

One woman patted my arm. "Honey, we know. It's just hard to be an independent woman with only one income. Maybe he'll come back. Lord knows you're pretty enough to make him rethink his options."

Another reached out for my collar and tugged at it, raking my neck with her nails in the process. "You need to wear something to make him remember that you're all woman."

I ran for the kitchen and found Mom standing in the very spot where Daddy ate his last meal, staring out the small window over the sink.

She glanced at me. "It's nice to see all of them, isn't it?" There was a lightness to her voice that didn't match the expression on her face. The frown from the funeral was there.

"Absolutely. When are they leaving?"

She laughed. "Now, baby, let them talk. They only get together at funerals these days. They have a lot to catch up on."

"Do they have to do it here?"

Her gaze settled back on the view out the window. "Weddings and funerals are for the people left behind, never for the people doing the deed." I watched my mother carefully, looking for the disappointment to appear on her face. My mother didn't discuss weddings with me. I had eloped and cheated her out of the big wedding that she'd been planning for me since I was born. I'd done a runner to Vegas in the hours between her evening news and her morning show and had an Elvis impersonator be the witness for my nuptials. This was as close to the subject we'd ever gotten since my return from Vegas when, breathless and ecstatic, I'd shown her my ring. Daddy had smiled and clapped Sam on the back, welcoming him to the family. Mom, however, looked at my teeny, tiny diamond and its matching band and said, with tears in her eyes, "Getting married is the easy part of love."

After that, she erected a barrier of cool politeness. Think Superman's ice fortress or Han Solo in carbonite. For months, she treated

Sam and me as if we were guests in her home. She served us drinks in her good crystal glasses—glasses I'd never been allowed to look at, much less touch, in all of my years on earth. For Sunday dinners, she pulled out her blue china, which was only exposed to the air for those rare family get-togethers when Grandma Kate was present. She'd been dead for years. Mom refused help from anyone who wasn't Daddy and wouldn't allow him to let us do anything either. It was awful.

This went on until Sam stopped her forward momentum one evening and swept her up in one of his full-body hugs, a hug that left you breathless and elated and with the knowledge that you are loved. He lifted her up off her feet and whispered to her, "Please, Mrs. Wilson, I love your daughter." My father and I only watched with our mouths open and drinks held aloft, frozen in their ascent to our mouths. He put her down after several long minutes. Mom smoothed her skirt and apron, looked up at him, and said, "Come help me with the dishes." And, like that, Sam was a favorite.

I took this conversation as tacit forgiveness and snuggled up next to her, forcing her to put an arm around me. She kissed my cheek. We stared out the kitchen window at the snowless roofs backed by a gray December sky.

—— •◦• ——

Six months later, Mom called me at 2:00AM crying, convinced loneliness would kill her. She'd dreamed about Daddy dying again. She explained how she'd woken up clutching the sheets around her as if she was trying to hold on to something—anything.

"He was there in full color," she told me, sniffling still. "Then he was face down on the floor, all black and white. Like the Technicolor ran away from him. His favorite cup was in pieces on the floor.

Remember the golf-ball-shaped mug? His dead fingers were still curled around the broken handle." She cried some more and told me she didn't want to die alone.

She asked me to move back home. I should've said yes, but I countered with, "Try something new. Join a club or find a hobby. Do anything to get out of the house." Within a week, she found a group, Lesbians over Forty.

"They are so nice, pumpkin. And they have group dance classes."

I questioned her. Why this club? "Aren't you interested in dating? Finding some companionship."

"I am. Some of those women are attractive," she said. I stared at her, and she laughed. "Baby, I didn't marry your father without some life experience."

I started to ask another question, but she cut me off. "I'm trying something new," she said with the steeliness in her voice I knew well. She had used it on me enough in my own childhood. She had taken my advice, and if I knew what was good for me (i.e., dinner delivered three nights a week and pot roast on Sunday,) I'd be quiet now.

———•—

By July, the engineering firm where I worked had been bought, and I was unemployed. With Sam gone, my apartment's rent had gone from affordable to tight-but-manageable to impossible. Sam called while I was packing. When I answered the phone, he said, "Don't hang up."

I waited.

"Marissa?"

"I'm waiting for the reason I shouldn't hang up," I said.

All around me were boxes full of books I never read and T-shirts I never wore. In the kitchen I'd found three blenders, two still in their boxes. They were given to us during the post-elopement wedding reception my mother insisted we have. The gift receipts were still taped to the boxes. I'd meant to exchange them, but Sam was sure we'd need them, so into the cabinet they went, back into a dark and dusty corner where spiders and unused Bundt pans resided.

"I just wanted to hear your voice." Sam sounded so defeated I couldn't hang up. I went to the fridge and from way in the back pulled out a bottle of his favorite beer. I popped the top and toasted a framed picture of us. I didn't have the heart to maim in some cathartic way. I sat down at the kitchen table and asked how his new city was treating him.

"Fine. The job is killing me, though." He'd been hired to write code for phone apps, but then the company merged with another company, and now he was writing code for other things. "Which is cool," he said, which I knew translated into I miss my old life.

"You wanted to move."

Sam groaned. I drank the beer. He had lived in Illinois all of his life. But when we broke up, he decided he needed something new. New sights, new apartment, and a new girlfriend, I assumed.

"I wanted a lot of things," he said quietly.

"Well, you got San Francisco, and I got Bardot." I tried to sound flippant, but I couldn't pull it off. Bardot, our almost two-year-old American Standard bulldog, came running at the mention of her name and sat down next to me, her mismatched eyes, one blue and one brown, looked at me hopefully.

"Look, I should go. Thanks for still being there," he said.

"I'm here all week," I said, trying for lounge-singer bravado. Part of me hoped he'd never call again, but that part was so infinitesimal it didn't matter.

"I miss you, Marissa."

"Bardot misses you," I told him. We hung up, and I finished the beer and my packing.

———•—•———

After a year of being divorced, I shifted into a long period of dating men who didn't interest me. Tall men, short men, skinny men who wore skinny jeans, bearlike men who favored flannel or Armani. I avoided men who reminded me of Sam: medium-size men with golden-blond hair who stood five foot ten, men who were computer savvy and overly gadget hungry.

There was Vincent, a friend of a friend. He was short, dark, and hairy in the best way, and he owned a failing bar in the west suburbs. At dinner, the conversation was awkward. He liked the Sox. I liked the Cubs. He hated office environments, and I couldn't wait to find a new office job. When dinner arrived, burgers and fries and a third beer for each of us, he said, "Can I touch your hair?"

I stopped chewing. "What?"

"I heard that black women don't like to have their hair touched," he said. There was a splotch of mustard at the corner of his mouth.

I swallowed and wiped my own. "So you asked me to see if it was true?"

"Yeah," he said. He took a long drink of his Tecate. "I guess that sounds . . ."

"Yeah, it kind of does. Have you ever asked a woman that before?"

"Well, no."

"Why, exactly, did you ask me out?"

"I've never dated a black girl before, and you're cute." Pause. "I meant sexy. Cute?"

My face must have been throwing him off. I wasn't sure quite what I was feeling at that moment. But I knew the date was over.

I met a guy at the dog park when Bardot ran away from me to sniff the butt of a Jack Russell who promptly began shaking and peeing where it stood. I apologized to the Jack Russell's owner, who told me the dog, whose name was actually Jack, had some trauma, and big dogs like Bardot terrified him. Bardot chased after a ball and Jack the dog calmed down. Jack's owner asked me for my number. Later it turned out that Jack's owner was also a pee-er. At least I knew now that golden showers were not on my personal fetish list.

For a couple of months, I dated a land surveyor who'd recently broken up with his wife. He favored semipublic hand jobs under restaurant tablecloths and sex in the backseats of cars, usually mine. Before our next date, he called to tell me he wanted to get back together with his wife, and I returned the wrist brace I'd just bought.

Then there was Clay, a nonpracticing lawyer I started talking to on the L one night. He was forty and DJ'd parties around Wicker Park and Wrigleyville. He stood six foot three and had a clean-shaven face with a big wide grin. I missed my stop talking to him. I got off at his, and he took me to his favorite pizza place where we had slices and beer and good conversation about everything but who we were. I went back to his apartment. He stripped me of my clothes and bounced me into his bed. I left teeth marks on his shoulder. Some neighbor pounded on a wall. After, we dressed, and Clay walked me to the train stop, paid to go up, and stayed with me until my train arrived. He kissed me as the train blew into the stop, and my heart, long since given up for dead, gave a little wobble in my chest.

Exhausted but giddy, I texted my friend Aiden. We'd known each other for years. We used to work at the same engineering firm. He was the one who told me things were worse than our bosses were telling us at the company meetings. He'd only survived the merger because he'd spent every bonus on company stock and it would cost too much to buy him out.

Marissa: Met a guy. The night was too short.

Aiden: did you google him before you slept with him?

Marissa: Why do you have to be so judgy? He was nice! :P

Aiden: so was Ted Bundy

So I googled my DJ-slash-not-lawyer-with-the-perfect-grin's name. Nothing crazy came up. On a whim, I typed his phone number into the search bar. I said, "Holy shit," out loud, but the three people in the train car with me didn't care about my outburst. Two were asleep, and one was vaping furtively and stabbing at his own phone with a shaky finger. On my phone were a dozen website links. AMATEUR BABES FUCKING! and HOT MILFS TAKING IT HARD!, the links said. All with Clay's phone number attached. I clicked the AMATEUR BABES link. I was diverted to a website called SECRET CAM VIDEOS. My heart stopped beating. I got off the train at the next stop, went down to the street, and then heaved myself up the opposite stairs to catch the train going the opposite direction.

Back at his apartment, which was over a Thai food restaurant, I leaned on his buzzer.

"Yeah?" He sounded tired. Must be from all that late-night editing he was doing. I had a vision of myself on my knees, breasts swaying underneath an uppercase headline that read BLACK GIRL FUCKING.

"It's me. I need to come back up." He buzzed me in. I climbed three flights of stairs, deciding what I'd say. Don't be aggressive. Be calm, be cool, I told myself. You're not a prude. You're not afraid of a little home video. I took a deep breath and knocked on his door. When he opened it, I slapped him.

"Where is it?" I pushed past him and started searching his tiny apartment.

"Where's what?" He was too shocked to be angry, yet I figured I only had a couple of minutes before that wore off.

"You seemed so nice. So normal," I said, overturning his laundry basket.

"So did you. What the fuck?" He pulled me away from his closet and made me look at him.

"Did you record us?"

A little line formed between his dark eyebrows. "What? How did you . . . ? No. I would've asked you," he said.

"Really?" I pulled my arms away and folded them over my chest.

"God, yeah. It's fucking illegal to do it without permission."

"I googled your number."

"Why?" He looked hurt. I noticed he wasn't wearing a shirt or socks, only sweatpants that hung off his hips sexily.

"You seemed so great, but I always check. Usually before." Oh, the lies.

"I never would have done that to you." He moved over to the bookshelf by his bed and showed me the camera. It was behind the books and under a fine layer of dust. "I haven't felt like adding to the site in a while." He shrugged. Somehow I took this to mean he thought I wasn't worthy enough to join the ranks of the women he'd recorded before. I was oddly disappointed.

"Fine, I believe you. But don't call me," I said. Then I pushed past him again and slammed his front door shut. It was a long, dark walk to the train. From then on, any guy I was interested in came back to my place. Still risky, but I wouldn't have to worry about some entrepreneur trying to add me to his site or a wannabe Aronofsky or Nolan trying to make his first film with me in it.

My dates coincided with Mom's new dating routine. She'd joined a dating service through L over Forty, and three times a week I heard about the latest woman to ask Mom out. Then she'd ask me about my dates. She wanted to trade stories as if we were girlfriends. Not mother and daughter. I declined. She told me hers anyway.

There was Elaine, a manager at Costco, who took Mom fishing in Carbondale. She only lasted two outings because Mom drew the line at camping. Then there was Monica, a sommelier, who was forever trying to get Mom to smell the wine and appreciate it. Mom confessed she was a wine drinker, not a wine sniffer. Monica didn't call again. Rochelle was a thirty-five-year-old yoga instructor. She took Mom to the Field Museum on their date. They laughed, had wonderful conversation, and Rochelle kissed her lightly at the door when she dropped her off at home. Mom politely asked her not to call again. When I asked why, Mom said, "The whole time we were together, I had an urge to ask what her mother's name was. I was sure I knew her from the neighborhood." Subsequent checking confirmed that Rochelle was the daughter of Mom's PTA nemesis. "It's for the best. She was too young, and can you imagine her introducing me to Doreen?" We both laughed at that.

Then a mere eighteen months after Daddy died, Mom found Margie.

Margie was curvy and wore power suits. Every day her dark-brown hair was up in a French braid. A dash of imperfectly applied red lipstick was all the makeup she could stand to wear. She was an accountant. My mother adored her. And for a long time, Margie adored her too. Margie and I grew to be good friends during the year they were together. Often we ate lunch together at her office downtown. We were so close that I knew before Mom did that Margie was unhappy.

"I thought the shine would wear off," Margie said. We were at a café near her office building. She flagged down our waitress and ordered another coffee with Baileys in it.

"What do you mean by shine?" I asked.

"Your mother always wants to go to Lesbian Disneyland and ride every ride. Let's go to that new bar opening, don't forget to wear the pink triangle pin I bought you. Or *Kissing Jessica Stein* is playing at the indie theater, let's go see it. Or, for fuck's sake, on the L, the hand-holding and trying to make out like she's a teenager. I'm fifty-five, Marissa, I don't need to perform to prove who or what I am."

Sitting across from Margie, I thought of the frown my mother had worn for over a year. Its absence now. I felt I needed to defend my mother from her accusations. "She's new to all this. She likes you a lot."

It was a limp defense. I knew my mother could be obsessive and impulsive. During my childhood, she tried any number of things to entertain herself: quilting, running, bridge, poker, canasta, bonsai tree trimming, jujitsu, and t'ai chi. These activities occupied her full attention for months at a time, until one morning she'd wake up and decide she was done with that and she was on to the next thing. She'd been a happy housewife, but nothing, except for Daddy and me, seemed to keep her attention for long. Daddy thought she was adventurous. I came to believe she was just quirky. Margie seemed to think my mother had a fatal flaw. After a year together, I'd figured they'd worked these things out between them. I was wrong, and Margie was gone by June.

During the weeks that followed, Mom mourned Margie as she had never mourned Daddy. It was as if she'd given up on life itself for a while. She let her hair go gray and wavy with new growth. I'd come over to check on her, and she'd be shuffling through the house in Daddy's old robe, smelling of Vicks VapoRub and stale cigarettes. Her eyes were perpetually red rimmed. She looked closer to seventy-five than sixty. I'd bring her soup and rub her feet. I'd listen to her tales of when she and Margie did this and that and sometimes, hopped up on cold medicine, she'd slur her way through a story about Daddy. But each night, it was Margie's name on her lips when she slipped off to sleep.

My mother's misery pushed me into action. I needed to get serious about dating, and I let Aiden set me up. "Someone low-key," I said.

"Trust me," he said.

The next week Aiden threw a surprise birthday party for his wife, Julie. She didn't like me much. Once, a very long time ago, so long ago, in fact, I would lump it together with puberty and wearing braces, Aiden and I had a marathon make-out session in the back booth of a dark bar; no hickeys were left, and we never did it again. The night before their wedding, Julie had insisted they come clean on everything. No secrets. Nothing that could show up and put a wedge between them. He overshared, and from then on, she glared at me every time she saw me. Even when I was still married, she watched me. Now I was divorced, she got to rise above me in the marriage category and up her suspicion level from yellow to orange anytime I was near.

At their two-story Craftsman home, situated in the north suburbs of Chicago, the 2.5-kids-and-a-dog-ready yard was full of balloons and streamers in her favorite colors, black and red—bordello colors, my mother would've tsked—and forty birthday well-wishers, including my blind date and I, were all waiting for her to show up.

My blind date's name was Josh. He had wide-spaced brown eyes. His breath smelled like Heineken. The only thing he had in common with my ex-husband was that he was white too. He was thirty-five and had been abandoned at the altar. "Not that I'm angry or anything," he whispered into my ear.

"Why be angry?" I said. "My husband left me too. Not at the altar, but he left."

He leaned closer. "The bastard."

"I knew you'd understand." We laughed.

Inside the house, a light came on. We all quieted down. Another light turned on and spilled across the back porch. The back door opened, and Aiden and Julie appeared. Her eyes were closed. A wide grin graced her pretty, tanned face. He maneuvered her to the center of the porch, facing all of us. Then he came down the steps, turned, and said, "Okay, one, two, three!" Strands of lights crisscrossing the yard blinked on. We all yelled Happy Birthday. Josh grabbed my hand, slipped his fingers between mine, and we all sang to her. It was lovely and sincere, and I was the happiest I'd been since before Sam left. Aiden hugged Julie. It was a party. There was love in the air.

Two hours in, my purse gave a feeble tremble. My cell phone was dying. The last message it gave was that I had four voicemails waiting. Then the screen went dark.

"Need to borrow mine?" Josh asked, already pulling his phone from the holster on his belt.

"It's okay. I have messages I need to get. I'll use Aiden's phone."

Josh reached out, brushed his fingers across my cheek and down my neck. I felt a stupid smile bloom on my face. I turned away so he wouldn't see it.

———•◦•———

In their house, next to the perfectly appointed dining room with a full china cabinet and a mahogany table with its twelve matching chairs was Aiden's office. On one wall hung his fifty-five-inch flatscreen television with his gaming systems and library of video games on shelves beneath it. I went to his glass-topped desk and sat behind it. Sitting there, I missed my old office and my own desk with its own many-buttoned phone. I shook off my desk envy, found paper and pen, then pressed the speaker button on his desk phone and dialed into my voicemail.

The first two messages were from temp agencies and another

from a headhunter wondering how I felt about working in Dubai. I wrote down the numbers and names so I could google them later. The fourth message was from my landlady, Tina.

"Ms. Wilson, I know you're probably working," she said in her high, nasally voice. Tina was my age but sounded like a grandmother. "But I've had some complaints about you." She paused. Here, I thought of my neighbor, the creepy guy with the überskinny mustache. He'd asked me out, then scratched his balls, a lot, right there in front of me. All I could think was that not even when she had fleas Bardot had never scratched that much. I'd said no. He was offended and called me a bitch. As Tina continued, Aiden and Julie walked into the office with Josh. They waited while Tina got to her point.

"Perhaps you could, I don't know, put up curtains maybe? It's just, you've been having sex, and the whole building has witnessed it. And not that I would judge, but it's rarely the same man twice. Mrs. Klein in 4B wonders if you're a call girl or something, which, I have to tell you, you can't do in our building, Ms. Wilson." I pounded on the release button, but Tina went on for another sentence or two before the call hung up. Aiden and Josh laughed uncomfortably. Julie actually looked sorry for me. Then she wrapped her arms around Aiden and smiled at me.

I considered telling them about my new L-shaped apartment building and my tiny new apartment, which had two windows, and how, desperate for natural light, I left these windows curtainless. The windows faced out on to rooftops of other buildings. I never worried about my neighbors looking into my place. Obviously, this was a mistake. I left the birthday party early. Josh never called.

A week after the birthday party, I fell asleep on my mother's couch. I'd been hiding at her house since my landlord's call, though I hadn't told my mother why. She seemed happy to have me in the house.

She could beat in dominos and drink her evening wine. During her midnight shuffle to the bathroom, she stopped and shook me awake. "Why are you asleep on my couch?"

Her couch was a new addition bought during the last outing with Margie. Mom barely let me sit on it most days, but that night I had settled into it to read, leaned back into the plush newness of the couch, and fell asleep, the book unopened on the cushion next to me. Mom went to the bathroom. At her return, she nudged me over and put her slippered feet onto my lap. She was wearing Margie's red velour slippers.

"You okay, Mom?" I rubbed her feet.

"Peachy, baby." She yawned.

"You want to talk about it?" All this time, I had avoided asking Mom directly about how she felt about Margie's leaving. I'd only wanted to be there for her.

"Nothing to talk about. I'll get over her soon enough," she said.

"Like you got over Daddy?" I heard my voice regress to that of my eight-year-old self. I didn't look at her, only kept rubbing her velour-covered feet until she pulled them from me and sat up.

"I didn't get over your father, Marissa." She took my hands in hers. "I miss him. I don't wonder about our future, but with Margie, I keep wondering."

"Wondering who made the mistake?" I said, thinking of Sam so far away. Almost two years later and I still wondered if the mistake was his for not staying or mine for not wanting what he wanted.

She nodded. Then she said, "Sometimes I say their names, out loud, I mean. Like I can invoke them or breathe a memory of them." Her voice hit a depth of sadness I had never heard before. My mother shook her head and looked down at her hands as if ashamed of this weakness of this need. But I still woke every day with thoughts of Sam on my mind and his name in my mouth, a stone weight on my tongue. Then I felt bad that I was thinking about Sam and myself when she was the one who needed me right then. So I told her about the call from my landlord.

"Mom, I have to sneak into my apartment building now. How can I look these people in the eye?" I said. "I keep imagining Mrs. Klein taking off her bifocals and looking into my apartment through her grandson's Boy Scouts–issued binoculars."

Mom snorted once, trying to keep the laughter to herself, but she couldn't help it. She let loose gut-deep laughter that rocked her whole body. I laughed with her. Laughter shifted into tears, and tears moved on into full-fledged sobbing. We held hands until we were both cried out.

Eight days later, Mom called to say she was done with all the crying, the shuffling, and the reminiscing. She told me she accepted it and wished Her the best. Which was how Margie was forever to be known: Her. Mom asked how I was. I was fine, I told her. Of course, her mom-radar was working once again. My voice told her everything she needed to hear about how I was really doing at that moment. I still hadn't found a full-time job. My savings were nearly gone. I told her I couldn't afford my car payment and rent.

"So let the car go then, baby. It's a big gas-guzzling car, much too big for you and the Bardot."

"I can't. What if Bardot gets sick? I'll need to take her to the vet."

Mom didn't say anything for a minute, just let my words hang between us. I knew how I sounded, but I was serious. Bardot was the only piece of Sam I had left, and I wouldn't risk her health.

"You'll meet someone else," she said.

"This isn't about Sam." I wiped my nose. My face was hot and swollen from the crying I'd been doing over my stupid SUV. Mom offered to pay off my car. I said yes. Then she recruited me as her dance partner. Together we spent the rest of the summer learning to ballroom dance. This was the last class that L over Forty offered after hip-hop, jazz, and tap. She and Margie had taken all those. Then she signed us up for the Fall Weekly Dance.

———•◦•———

On Monday nights we danced in the park. First, though, in the parking lot, we sat on the bumpers of our cars, waiting on the last of the dancers to arrive. Mom played hostess, and we played guests, and we all had coffee and donuts, or sometimes Mom brought her special rum-laced coffee cake. Mom mingled and cajoled the group into smiles and laughter. Then, as if she'd heard some alarm, she'd find me, place my hand in hers, and like a majorette at the start of some odd parade, she'd lead us all onto the wide concrete area used for music events there in the park.

The music was in French, courtesy of Ms. Renault, who tonight sat on the sidelines watching our steps with her partner, Marie. The song playing was "La Vie en Rose," and I suspected it was Ms. Renault doing the singing. Near Marie's feet sat Bardot, whose tail wagged each time I looked her way.

It was ten o'clock at night and Mom was wrapped up in her fleece jacket to fend off the early-October chill. I took her hand and led her out into the safe middle, out of the way of the more experienced dancers. If Margie had been here, she'd have Mom floating across the park, but my dancing abilities were limited. While couples danced around us with more sophisticated moves, Mom was content to dance my simple box step and whisper to me about the other dancers.

Miss Petrova and Mrs. Polyakova were easily the most elegant pair out tonight. Two round grandmothers in matching jackets, long skirts, and twin smiles of contentment who found each other again.

Miss Petrova was a dancer when she defected in the late seventies. Mrs. Polyakova tried to join her but was detained by the KGB and instead went on to marry Mr. Polyakov and bear him three sons. As soon as the USSR fell in 1991, she and her three sons escaped to the US, and by 1995, she and Miss Petrova were together. Now they are ballroom dancers once a week and grandmothers to a half-dozen grandkids. They smiled as they went by. They really wanted me to meet the youngest son, the single one. He has an art degree, Miss Petrova told me, her eyes rolling, but a good man. I smiled back at them as they swept past us.

I chanced a spin with Mom. The last time I tried, our coordination was off, and we both nearly fell over. She giggled this time.

"You're getting better," she said.

"I'm practicing."

"With who? Anyone I should meet?" She was a little desperate to meet my someone. I told her the truth: I practiced with a five-foot-tall stuffed bear won for me by a man I didn't see anymore. I didn't tell her this man had a wife and a thing for black women. We had sex twice. Both times, he brought with him a homemade DVD with pieced together clips of minimally dressed black women from rap videos, their asses moving in slow motion on my flat screen as he bent me over the back of my couch. I stopped taking his calls after he wouldn't stop spanking my ass during sex. He was apologetic on my voicemail, pleading and admitting that my ass was so perfect and round he just had to see it jiggle. I didn't see him again, but it was a close thing. I hadn't met anyone in the last three months worth seeing twice.

The Martins, Karen and Joanne, glided past us. Mondays were their date night. As they whisked off to the other end of the dance area, my mother said, "They have eight-year-old twins and infidelity issues." As if I didn't know. Karen was unable to stop herself from flirting with me. Once she told me, "I wonder how you taste," when she caught me by myself one Monday night.

Joanne apologized later. "It's a thing she does when she's nervous." Then she told me Karen said the same thing to her the night they met. I blinked at her. She shrugged. "It wasn't clever, but it was ballsy."

Celia and Rita danced stiffly. My mother smiled sadly at them. Celia usually wore her red hair in a high ponytail, though I saw it was much shorter now. My mother told me they fought last week over something silly, and Celia, angry and desperate, took her ponytail in one hand and a pair of scissors in the other hand and removed the long swoop of hair from the back of her head. Now, as they danced, Celia chewed on the ends of the chin-length strands that framed her face. When the couple turned, I saw the shorn back of her head. Actually, she looked quite nice with the severe cut. Celia, with her high cheekbones and slightly upturned nose, would be good-looking in a burlap sack, I decided. Even in her misery.

"Awful, I know," Mom said. "But they're no different than you and Sam or Margie and me."

Ms. Renault raised her hand. We all stopped. It was time to switch. Suddenly I had my arms full of Karen. Joanne was matched with Marie. A tango began to play. Karen grinned at me. "Come on, Marissa. We can do this."

We'd both been voted the worst dancers in the group. We lived up to it. We stumbled and giggled through the steps, hamming up the poses, my scarf in my mouth and our gazes locked in our best passionate looks. Mom found a willing partner in Miss Petrova. They were quite impressive. Miss Petrova's elegant footwork captured all our attention. We stopped to watch them. Mrs. Polyakova's hands hid her smile.

Celia watched from across the walkway. She looked away when she saw me notice her. "Don't mind her," Rita said.

"I'd hate to get in the middle of something," I said.

"You aren't. We were over before we started taking this class, but Celia . . ." Rita tilted her head and sighed. "I love Celia. She's great. But you can only give so much before it starts to hurt. You know?"

I guess I did know, though I wasn't in a mood to commiserate. I felt like I should take Celia's side. I said, "Maybe you shouldn't be dancing with her once a week. Maybe she needs some distance."

"What difference would it make? I can't afford to move out, so we're still in the house together," Rita said.

The song ended. We all clapped for Mom and Miss Petrova. The next song was another waltz. Ms. Renault called for another switch. Mrs. Polyakova started clapping and squealed, "Sasha!" and all eyes turned to see a man wrapping long arms around her and lifting her up off the ground. Miss Petrova was at my side in an instant. "Our Sasha, the artist," she said.

Mom waved at me. I waved back. She shook her head and waved at me again. She wanted me to have a meet-cute with Sasha. I smiled at Miss Petrova and let her introduce me to her son. He worked at the Art Institute. They convinced us to dance. Sasha spun me out onto the concrete and pressed me close. Into my ear, he said, "I have a girlfriend. They hate her."

"I think my heart's too broken or jaded or something to fall for someone else." He looked at me. "I didn't mean to say that," I said.

"You're a very good dancer," he said. I was doing waltz steps I'd never managed in class.

"I'm learning, I guess."

"You'll learn other things too. Have faith," he said.

I thought of Mom on the sidelines, swaying to the music, happy again even without Margie or Daddy, and Sam in San Francisco living without me.

"I do have faith," I said, and almost believed it.

Laundry

You like doing laundry. While your husband was in prison, doing the laundry became a cherished time. Waiting for clothes to wash and dry took your mind off the waiting for Bear. Clothes went in and would come out at a certain time. It was something you could look forward to and count on. However, now that he is home, doing the laundry has become a chore. Two people make much more laundry than one.

You go from bedroom to bathroom collecting the laundry, then plop them into heaps of clothes and towels across your tile floor, a miniature mountain range of cottons and polyesters. You can hear your mother berating you for your laziness. She did the laundry on Wednesday, every Wednesday of your childhood. She'd load the washer then smoke on the spin cycles, watching you play in your backyard with the hose or chase the dog. Then back in to pull the wet clothes into the dryer and set the timer. Then back out to have another cigarette.

However, you work, and there are no children to watch. There are no children at all, not that you mind. He's been gone so long, but now he is back, and you are happy. So, for you, laundry is done every two weeks, which is fine because you both have uniforms you wear and plenty of them to last for two weeks plus. This is good because last week you forgot to do laundry and now you are down to one too small pair of panties that you should have gotten rid of years ago, but you didn't, and now you're wearing them. Right now, the elastic band is cutting into you, cutting into the weight you put on in the years he has been gone. The weight has spread out across your hips, ass, and thighs, but he claims to like it, so you don't worry about it. Not too much.

Anyway, you gather and separate colors from the lights and from the darks and another level of separation because he likes it this way: the shirts from the pants from the underwear. You lobbied hard to get the socks combined with the underwear. Besides, you fold it and put it away; he will live with it, and he has. You check the pockets of shirts and then the pants, but halfway through you say the hell with it and throw it all in the washer, pockets unchecked. You just want to get it done.

You found him a job working for a mechanic. Within a month, your husband had the run of the place. That's Bear's way. He has a presence that could make anyone believe he was harmless and trustworthy. Of course, the man he killed might say differently, but he is dead, and Bear has served his time, and you try not to think about that.

Seven years is a long time. He's quieter than you remember. The gray hair he has now makes him seem older than his thirty-eight years. Not that you've fared much better serving your time out here. He's spent seven years looking out. You've spent seven years looking in. But he is home now.

The washer works its way through and hits the first spin cycle. You go outside to stand in your backyard. The home improvement bug has bitten Bear. He has worked these last two weekends stripping the ground because he wants grass. Tomorrow men will come to lay down sod. You look up at your big willow tree. He says it should go because it's too big, that it doesn't belong in this yard, in this part of the country even. If it were gone, he could put in a pool, but you've put your foot down, and the tree is staying. That tree was the sole reason you bought this tiny house. It had this tree and plenty of yard left over for children to play. Now he wants a Japanese koi pond. He doesn't want kids. He wants fish. He says he dreamed about fish while he was in prison. Dreamed about them swimming round and round just for him. You don't tell him what you think of that. Nor do you tell him that you have been dreaming of babies. Seven years worth of dreaming. He wants a koi pond. Therefore, he has dug a hole. The dirt from the hole is piled high next to your tree with the neighbor's borrowed shovel stuck in it, and the hole, it is too deep by your estimation, and you tell him this.

He says, "Are you the resident hole inspector?"

You keep your opinions to yourself. You don't smoke, but when you close your eyes, you can smell your mother's cigarettes. You can still see her squinting against the smoke, the corners of her eyes crinkled up. She'd like your tree.

———•—

Bear walked out of prison a short three months ago, and you were so happy. So happy you leaped and damn near clicked your heels. A dream made real when he slid his body, once round and pudgy—the reason why everyone called him Bear—now lean and hard from seven years inside, across the car's bench seat and kissed you. He shut the door and slammed his hand down on the lock once, then twice, as if making sure they couldn't come and drag him away from freedom. Then he turned to you and said, "Let's go home, sugar." You smiled, and just for him, you make the car fishtail in the gravel in front of that prison in Ely and listened to him laugh all the way to the state highway and home to North Las Vegas. Later that night, when he curled up close to you, his hands, rougher than you remembered, rubbed up and down thighs that were bigger than he surely remembered, and he whispered, "I'm never going back there. Never."

———— •◦• ————

You hear the washer switch gears—the rinse cycle—and you go back in. Eight minutes later, you are pulling the wet, cold clothes from the washer and into the dryer, placing a new load of dirty clothes—the colored shirts this time—into the washer. You set the dials, hit the buttons, grab your purse, and go to get your work shirts from dry cleaners before they close. You've left this errand for too late in the day, and traffic—snarled and crawling—is working against you. Eventually, you drift into Summerlin and pass the master-planned neighborhoods with their middle-class restaurants.

You see something, someone, and you'd swear it was your husband standing outside an open-air bar and eatery. So sure are you that you make a U-turn and go back to the bar. By the time you make it back, there are different people standing out front and on the sidewalk. You shake off the feeling that has begun to creep along your spine and U-turn again and head back up the street to the dry cleaners.

By the time you make it home, he should be there, but you are greeted by a silent house. You check the phone, MESSAGE WAITING flashes at you. You put the phone down and rush into the laundry room, tending to the clothes as if they are forgotten children and you are their wayward mother. However, you're in luck; they are fine and not too wrinkled from your neglect. Some are still a little damp, so you reset the timer.

"Hey, babe," the message from your husband, the ex-convict who manages the local mechanic's garage, begins "working late. Don't wait up."

———•—•—•———

Your first visit, while he was in jail, was at the detention center downtown. You were so worried about him in there. Every version of every TV jail scene ran through your mind while you waited for visiting hours to begin. You were positive it was worse than TV. You waited your turn in line, then walked the down the long row of chairs searching for him. Each chair faced a plexiglass window with a matching chair on the other side, the detainee's side. Empty chair, empty chair, then Bear—his round face broadcasting a smile at you. For a moment, it was as if you and he were just sitting down at a table like the one in the bar where your nightmare started. He leaned back as far as he could and still managed to talk on the phone that carried his voice to you.

"It's cool," he said, "I mean it smells like, eh, you don't even want know." He chuckled like it was nothing, him being there. His grin widened. You focused on his lips. How they curved up into that smile you love. The thin upper lip and its full bottom counterpart. You liked to bite that bottom lip when you kiss him, to nibble on it while his hands roamed across you. And then you were crying deep, choking sobs and you heard him distantly over your sobs. "It'll be okay, baby. You'll see. Don't cry." He put his hand flat against the glass, beckoning you. You matched his gesture, your hand twinned with his, and there it is. The promise—It'll be okay.

Your time went that first visit quickly, but you got up when your half hour was done and waved goodbye to him. You hadn't noticed the other men at first, but now, you did. The men looked out from behind their plexiglass barriers like lost dogs waiting for their owners to come for them. They stared at the backs of their people, disappointment on their faces as the door swung closed behind each one and then behind you. The next time you came, Bear had that same look. He was found guilty; the gavel came down and seven years was your punishment.

———— •●•— ————

You stand in your backyard and look up at your favorite tree and his hole, and that feeling rises up again, but the buzzer goes off—time to fold the clothes. You hang the shirts (you'll iron his later) and fold your own. You upend your pants, line up the hems, and drape them over hangers. Then you assess his pants. You see that they will need to be ironed too, but for the moment, you just upend his pants too and begin hanging them. It is the third pair that contains the problem. The needle in the haystack of his promises. Turned upside down and sharply jerked straight, a wad of white paper falls out of the pants pocket and lands at your feet. You hope it isn't something important, like a receipt for some part that his office will end up needing. He does things like this all the time, forgetting things in his pockets, which is why you always check, but you were too tired this time, so you didn't check and here you are. The paper is folded and smushed. Tinted blue and gray from ink, it's still a little damp, but you can unfold it. You hope there is something salvageable on it, but what there is reads,

ecca

1 4172

Ecca? You ponder this fragment, then you understand. The feeling is back. It swamps you with the memory of the man downtown, the one you thought was your husband. That man with his hand on the small of some blonde-haired woman's back. The man who was gone when you turned around to look again.

You decide to wait up for him.

One hour creeps into the next. The laundry beckons you. You strip your bed of its sheets and the pillows of their cases. Three months of having him in your bed after such a long absence. His arm around your waist and his leg stretched out across your two locks you firmly in place nightly. He grounds you with his firm mass. Keeps you here and lets you breathe; lets you slowly release the breath you've held since before the verdict came down and your shared sentence was declared. Now you have him every night, just like he promised in letters and phone calls. It'll be okay, he said. But you know it isn't.

——•◆•——

You excused yourself that night at the bar and swayed to the bathroom. When you came back out, Bear wasn't at your table, but you spotted him with a blonde at the pool tables. You watched as he leaned in close and said something only for her. She grinned, flipped her hair over her shoulder, then she looked at you, and her smile faded. But it wasn't you she recognized. You heard a man curse. As you turned to look, he brushed past you, stalking towards Bear and the blonde. Bear smiled and backed away, hands and beer up in surrender. You took in a breath. The guy was a little too slow. Bear was just a little too good, though even he was surprised when the man didn't rise again. The blonde wept over her boyfriend and Bear stood over them, looking down at what he had done. And you only watched, not breathing still, and it's like you haven't breathed since.

You remember Bear's face, so uncomprehending. His eyes wide, he turned his head left, then right, searching, and then he found you. He always found you. He sank to his knees next to the fallen man and looked at you. In a moment, you were at his side and your fingers in his soft hair. You pushed away from the feeling rising in you—the fear—and forgave him, at that moment. He had been foolish. But you are the fool's wife.

———— •●• ————

You call the locksmith; "24 hrs at the ready" said the ad, and they were good on their word. In the time it took for the sheets to wash and get halfway through their drying cycle, you had new keys, and the locksmith had even been kind enough to show you how to disconnect the garage opener.

"Until you get the code changed." He smiled at you, pity in his eyes as if he knew; he probably did. How many locks had he changed for wives of fools? Too many, you are certain. On the front door, you tape Rebecca's phone number (you've figured out that much) with a note: I found this in your pocket; I thought you might need it. You turn on the porch light so he'll be sure to see it.

It is late when he comes home. You hear him drive up when you are in the backyard. You've been listening to the wind rustle the leaves of your tree while you stand over his hole with a flashlight. You still think the hole is too deep for a pond. You creep into the house, set the locks in the back door, and reach the front door in time to hear his key try to find its home in the lock. No home for his key. The locksmith took its home with him. You press your ear to the door and hear a muffled word. A knock at the door, tentative at first, sends you scrambling away. Then he pounds against it. He begins yelling your name, apologies, "misunderstanding," "please," your name again.

———— ·•· ————

He was at the state prison for weeks before you could go see him. You kept expecting him to call, but he didn't. Finally, you arrived with the others: mothers, fathers, girlfriends, and wives like you. You were searched, then you waited. A dozen men walked out. Tears were shed by mothers, and fathers, the bulk of whom looked angry, sat by their wives as they gushed. All of the men looked at you; their faces were hard. Their gazes set your skin crawling. Mingled irritation and fear ran along the inside of your arms. They watched you as you sat waiting, alone in the back of the room, like hungry animals, no longer showing the fear they must have once felt, the fear you had seen in Bear's face and felt in your own heart. Then Bear emerged, bruised but swaggering nonetheless. And you saw the same hungry look in his eyes. You knew he had changed then, but you ignored it and smiled for him. And like the others, he watched the room looking for their weaknesses. You promised him that day that you'd wait for him. You kept your promise. He could spend time waiting now, like you did.

The dryer ends its cycle. The buzzer goes off. You take the phone, turn off all the lights, and head into the laundry room. Setting the timer again, you climb up on top of your washer and dryer, duck your head under the shelf, and lean back to listen to the rhythm of the dryer and his pounding at the door.

Mendelson in the Park

On our last night together, we tango in the park. This doesn't happen often. While Mendelson doesn't have a problem dancing in the safety of our living rooms or at the studio with our teacher Ms. Renault circling and correcting us, in public he'd rather be a watcher, a toe-tapper, an ass-in-chair wiggler. I can count on one hand how many times he's danced with me where someone could possibly see us. There was one time during our summer when I talked him into dancing the cha-cha in his backyard, both of us in our underwear, fireflies lighting the night.

We've spent twenty months apart, trading long letters and smiling into laptop cameras at each other. Now he's barely been home a month. It's my unit's turn to rotate out. Between his family and friends welcoming him home and my mother and friends trying to say goodbye, we've hardly seen each other, and tonight he's supposed to be driving me to the base, but instead, we're here dancing. We'd make Ms. Renault so proud.

It's just this side of too cold, but I'm warm enough in my uniform. Mendelson is in a dark wool suit looking finer than I've ever seen him, which is saying a lot because I spent sixty-three summer days in bed with him, and he looks quite fine when naked. My boot drags a scuff across the toe of his shiny black dress shoe, and we stumble to a stop.

"Sorry, new boots," I say.

He gives me his patented half smile: head tilt left, and the right side of his mouth rises to reveal a hint of dimple visible in the park's lamplight. We start again, hip and thigh sliding against each other, his hand on my back. I lean my head on his chest for a moment. He smells clean and crisp, a mix of soap, shampoo, and starch. I want to press my nose into his neck and breathe deep. I want to carry his scent with me against the smell of the airports and the sweat of other soldiers and the dozen other smells that wait for me in the coming days and weeks, but I don't want to ruin the collar of his dress shirt with the tears that are threatening. I asked him about the suit when he showed up at my mom's, but he just shrugged and said he wanted to look good. By the time my tour is up to the smell of diesel and smoke, and the sound of mortar fire will have overwritten everything remotely domestic, so I let the question go unanswered and breathe him in.

"You ready?" he asks. For the desert, for the fear, for Afghanistan, he means. I am. I've been dreaming of my last tour for days now. Dreaming of long nights spent talking with Monroe, Batista, and Diaz in our tent about food, movies, and home. Monroe's main concern had been about the children she hadn't decided on having yet, so whenever she could, she'd get us talking about which of us took the pill or received a shot to manage our cycles and the reasons for our choices. Baptiste, Diaz, and I thought it was common sense given the heat and the dust and us pulling eight hours or more on our feet or hunkered down in convoy. Privacy and time weren't available in this man's army. Monroe was forever caught up trying to analyze the long-term effects of suppressants on our bodies. I tried never to worry about anything more than three months out. Three months was the exact amount of time between my Depo shots. Three months from now, I'll be bunked in some other corner of Afghanistan trying to stay warm at midnight and avoiding IEDs during the day. On patrol, I'll be walking through villages where the US Army is not wanted, meeting the eyes of women who are forbidden to talk to male soldiers. Trying to convince these women that we are friends. To convince them that we are not their enemy and to get them to tell their men the same. I will say, How can I help you? again and again. It's all I know how to say in Pashto, that and Stop or I'll shoot. In three months, I will be doing my job in Afghanistan. I will be a better version of me in Afghanistan.

"I'm sure you'll only be running some VIP from point to point. You'll keep him safe, and they won't send you out too far into trouble," Mendelson says. Our tango has devolved into swaying and shuffling feet.

I tell him, "Not that I actually need to go far to find trouble, Mendelson." He tightens his hold on me and rests his cheek against my temple.

Four years ago, an IED flipped the vehicle I was in. The doors wouldn't open, and we were taking fire from all sides, it seemed. I spent the longest ten minutes of my life in the hot, dim confines of a Humvee trying to return fire while upside down with blood dripping into one eye from a cut on my lip. We were lucky that day, my team and the journalist and the interpreter. We made it out with only two seriously wounded and no dead. Mendelson knows this story. He knows all my stories.

We met in Kandahar three years ago, eyed each other while our COs talked and laughed. Twice more, our paths crossed before Mendelson was injured and shipped out. Nothing important was said between us. The usual where-have-you-served and do-you-know-this-soldier small talk. There was a pull every time he was near me, though, a different kind of gravity that made me sway his direction. He told me later that he called in every favor owed to find out if I'd made it through my tour okay.

Then we met again in late June, at a rec center in the suburbs of Chicago. Mendelson was there with his grandmother and a gaggle of other grannies when my uncle and I entered the dance studio. My uncle needed to learn how to waltz before he married for the third time. I was the only person in our family he trusted not to tease him about the lessons. If Mendelson hadn't been in his camouflage uniform that day, I wouldn't have recognized him. He'd let his hair grow out, and there was an ease to his posture that said he was comfortable in his skin and in this civilian world, an ease I never quite seem to find when I'm home.

His grandmother made him wear his camo so everyone could see her handsome grandson in his army finery. Her friends clustered around him, cooing and making plans for him to meet their granddaughters and great-nieces. My uncle went off to find Ms. Renault, and I watched Mendelson work the old ladies. He grinned and shrugged, said Aw, shucks, in the all the right places, and then he saw me and his face went blank. I nodded hello, and he raised an eyebrow at me, then he tilted his head and gave that half smile of his.

It was two hours before we were alone. It was three hours before we were naked. We had thirty-two days together before he got word he was being shipped back to the heat, the sand, and the unpredictability that is Afghanistan. We made the most of the next thirty-one.

———•●•———

"Marry me," Mendelson says. I jerk my head off his chest and look at him. "You'll be gone eighteen months, and when you come back, in one piece,"—his voice hardens when he says this, and I note the warning and the plea. "I want you to come home to me."

"Mendelson." I shake my head, let go of his hand, and try to step away from him, but he holds on, dancing still.

His cheek is a little rough against mine when he leans in. His breath is warm in my ear when he says, "What? You don't love me?"

"I wish," I say, pulling my face away to look past his shoulder at the empty park around us. The path we're dancing on winds away into darkened recesses of the park, and it takes nothing for me to imagine that behind that stand of trees is a plain of crops that stretches to a river nestled against the foot of a mountain and that that sound of the helicopter in the far distance is a Chinook coming home. I'm nearly there. Mendelson kisses me, light and quick.

"So you love me, then," he says, and I can hear the smile as he pulls me close again and we take eight steps together. Our tango is so sloppy.

Mendelson knows I love him snoring next to me like a freight train through the night, my own personal white noise machine. I love the sound of his voice echoing over the seven thousand miles between us and seeing the relief on his face when he sees me on Skype after weeks of missed calls. I love the sight of his handwriting on the envelopes of the letters he sent me, one for nearly every week he was gone. I packed the best of them in my duffel to reread when I get over there. And I love the slide of his lips on my own, like the slide of our bodies. Oh, how I love.

During our summer, he told me about his father. How in the days before he died they finally began to talk. His father didn't apologize for years of perceived neglect; Mendelson didn't expect an apology. His father said I love you the way some men do: praise for athletic accomplishment—Mendelson had been a swimmer; he placed in the state championship his senior year of high school. His father hadn't wanted his boy to be coddled, so he never went to a meet but made his wife report on each race to him. He'd been proud of his son. His son, however, could say I love you; he wouldn't care who was in the room, and he said it every time he talked to his father until the cancer ended the phone calls. Mendelson could have gone home to attend the funeral, but he couldn't leave his battle buddies. He stayed in the Korengal Valley, watched his friends go KIA, and mourned them and his father both. This is the kind of man he is.

I tell him that we can talk about this later, when I get back from over there. He looks away from me and the muscles of his jaw flex. I remember us naked on my bed in front of the fan, the windows open to the sweltering heat of July, and us listing all the places we could go with air-conditioning.

A movie theater, I said.

You, me, and every teenager in the city, he said.

Lake Michigan boat cruise?

Tourists.

Bookstore?

I hate B&N.

He turned over and took the end of my ponytail in hand, twisting its length around his fist. He told me he loved the feel of it in his hand, sleek and strong like my body. Then his tongue was in my mouth, and we didn't go anywhere that day.

Now he stops our dance. "Sarge, hear me out."

"I can't, Mendelson." I pull away from him. Distance is good. I'm at the edge of a puddle of lamplight, my feet half off the walkway. I can feel the softness of earth under my heels. The light makes a halo around his head.

"I'm not re-upping," he says. "You're going to do your tour, then you'll be back. I want you with me." His arms drift wide. His fingers flex as if he's trying to hug me over two and a half feet of space.

"I am with you."

He frowns and shoves his hand in his trouser pockets.

I say, "Can't this wait until I come back? A ring isn't going to make me bulletproof, Mendelson. This can wait." I step back into his space and tilt my face up to his. His lips are cold, but his tongue is oh so hot, and I am breathless for a moment. I wonder what it would have been like if we'd gone back over there together. Would we have obeyed regs or snuck off for frantic lovemaking under cover of shadows? Would we have been the captain and the sergeant over there, or would we have been us?

He takes me in his arms again. We find a new position. A waltz. All our dances have waltzes in them somehow. The waltz is the foundation for everything we learned over our summer. "I want a life, sarge." I nod. He's so confident. So damn sure about what he wants. I know he'll be fine in this life. I can see it all so clearly for him, how it will all go.

He will make a life outside of the military and hold on to it with both hands because he's seen how easily life can end. I can see it all for him: He'll finish law school and be hired by a medium-sized law firm where he'll shine. He'll buy a condo or a townhouse in the city, walk to work when the weather's good, take a cab when it's not. He'll work hard and make partner before he's forty-five, not the youngest to do it but the fastest. At home, he'll have a toddler and one on the way and a wife who'll love to be home but she'll miss adult conversation so at night after little Mendelson is in bed they'll talk about the house, the kid, the baby, vacations, holiday plans, their mothers, and all the other minutiae of their life together.

But that wife is not me. I cannot do without the low thrum of diesel engines, the familiar sound of a few hundred soldiers all breathing near me. All of us waiting for the next round of mortar fire, for the next convoy across a kill zone in the middle of the night.

His eyes are on me, flicking over my face, mapping its terrain. I see when his eyes catch on the scar on my upper lip. He makes it a point to kiss me there every chance he gets, like his love can heal it and make me whole. Mendelson is a good man. He knows I twitch when alone in my apartment, jumping at the slightest noise, and the names of the three bars in town I'm banned from for fighting. It's not enough just to tell a guy to go away; I have to push him. Then he gets in my face. I don't let anyone get that close to me. Except for Mendelson.

He knows my mother wants me to see a therapist, but he doesn't push it, and that my father won't acknowledge me as long as I'm enlisted. The other day, when my father and I saw each other on the street, his eyes moved over me, then off, like I was a stranger. It's been that way for six years and isn't going to change anytime soon.

Standing with Mendelson in the park, I realize there isn't any salvaging to be done here. I will not, cannot, leave the military. Who am I, if not Staff Sergeant Vaughn? He nods his head slowly, like he can hear my thoughts. No one listens to me quite like he does. He comes close again. His lips brush against my forehead. His arm slips around me. We fall into positions for a box-step waltz. His right foot slides forward, my left foot slides back, then to the side and together.

"David," I say.

"You'll still call me."

Not a question. I nod.

We do a quarter turn, then another and another until I'm dizzy, and I shut my eyes. Weeks from now, when the transport plane sets us down in the desert and we report in, that first night under that deep black sky where there's no light pollution to hide the stars, I know I will remember tonight. The cool wind against my face, the low rustle of leaves, the wool of his suit under my fingertips, the solidness of his bicep under my hand, and the sound of his shoes scraping on the concrete walkway as he turns me for the last time. I will remember all of that and not what will come later: the drive to Indiana and into the parking lot of the base surrounded by the homes of the sleeping civilian masses, the Moms and Dads and their 2.5s all snug in their beds. There in the parking lot, Mendelson and I will say our goodbyes, and I will turn away, walk through the base's front door, and make myself not turn around to see him drive away.

Lucy Lucy Lucy

When Angela cornered Lucy in the girls' locker room and said "white girl," there was a moment when Lucy wanted to tell her how she wasn't white or black, only the perfect mix of both, which is what her father liked to say. Instead, she turned away as her mother had taught her. Her mother would say, "Don't fight. Be better than those petty girls, baby."

One of the LaLas, either LaDonnia or LaTasha, freshman girls who'd once been friends with Lucy, said, "Cut her hair," and laughed.

Lucy grabbed the long thick braids that trailed down her back and tried to think of a comeback—something, anything—but before she could, Angela turned her around, then pushed her hard. Lucy fell back against the metal lockers, her head colliding with a lock, the pain making brilliant spots of color in front of her eyes, and with that, Lucille Jones was done turning the other cheek.

Lucy swung first and kept swinging, her fists connecting with the body beneath her until Coach Daniels blew her whistle. Lucy stopped mid-swing, breathing hard. She stood and wiped her hand across her face. There was a long streak of vibrant red across the pale skin of her palm. She was bleeding but felt nothing other than the ecstatic beating of her heart.

On the floor, in the middle of a mess of backpacks and clothes and books, Angela was furious. She was still trying to kick Lucy as Coach pulled her away. Behind them, the LaLas stood, disbelief twitching off one girl's face and onto the other.

In the principal's office, each girl had a chance to explain what happened. Angela said Lucy started it, and that was all she had to say. Lucy calmly explained the situation and described the previous altercations, including the group teasing and the hair threatening, finishing with, "Then she pushed me into the lockers, Mr. Allegretti." The girls left the office and sat across from each other. Angela glared at her. Lucy wasn't worried until their mothers showed up.

The Lucy her mother wanted her to be had "good girl" friends. Friends who did their homework and didn't sass or roll their eyes. This Lucy told her parents about her good day at school, even though most days weren't good at all. At school, she kept her head down and tried to disappear. At school, there was nowhere for her to hide. She didn't fit anywhere. Pale as she was. Mixed like she was. Different as she was. These versions of Lucy were always on her mind.

Angela and her mother went into the principal's office first. While they waited in the hardback chairs, Lucy watched her mother carefully. She sat stiff and unmoving, like the collar of her uniform shirt. She had mentioned more than to Lucy once how much she hated the green polyester pants that hugged her hips and the patterned jungle shirt she had to wear for her job as a blackjack dealer at the Tropicana Casino. She didn't look at Lucy and seemed to be studying a banner in the hallway that read Tiffany Carter 4 Prom Queen - CLASS of 1988 RULEZ! in alternating primary colors.

"Nice girls don't fight," Lucy's mother finally said.

"She started it. She called me white girl," Lucy said too quickly.

Her mother's mouth tightened, but she didn't look at Lucy. "And she threatened to cut my hair."

Her mother loved her hair and frequently mentioned how lucky Lucy was because she wouldn't have to endure relaxers and hot combs like her mother had when she was a little girl. Honestly, Lucy didn't care much about her hair, which was long and, when not properly restrained in braids, expanded into wild curls. Most days she struggled to put it in manageable braids and occasionally a fat barrette.

Her mother turned to her, smoothed her hand over Lucy's face, covering her eyes until Lucy relaxed and leaned into her palm. Her mother lifted her hand and said, "Well, if she started it, then I can't blame you."

Lucy's mother argued down a two-week suspension to three days of detention citing her daughter's excellent grades and good behavior in the face of such obvious bullying, finishing with, "That girl provoked an altercation with Lucy. Now we need to think about what lesson needs to be learned here. The lesson is sometimes you have to fight back."

———•—•———

On the first afternoon of detention, there were five detainees including Lucy. A redheaded boy she didn't know made endless paper airplanes in different shapes and sizes. Lucy watched the planes fly for fractions of seconds then plummet to the floor. The others were the LaLas and a girl named Therese.

Therese was seventeen and still a sophomore. The story was she'd failed eighth grade, then managed to fail so many classes her sophomore year they couldn't let her become a junior. The better story was Therese's parents split up the summer before after a very public argument in the Lucky's grocery store parking lot, which ended with her mother being taken away in handcuffs for assault with a deadly weapon, namely her 1974 two-door, butter-yellow Subaru. Therese's father left town for a job in Ohio, and her mother, now on probation, worked nights and drank during the day. Therese was always in detention for one thing or another. She didn't seem to care what anyone thought of her.

Therese had a magazine spread out across her desk, and the girls were pointing at the pictures. The LaLas clustered around Therese like mosquitoes, their voices buzzing. Lucy could see the slick pages with models on them. Therese caught Lucy looking her way.

"Hey you," Therese said. The LaLas turned to look at Lucy, matching dark looks on their faces.

Lucy gave a little smile to Therese and looked out the window at the school practicing on the field. There was a squeal of metal against linoleum and Lucy turned back to see Therese weaving slowly between the desks. Her hair, done up in small braids with pink beads twisted in, brushed her shoulders. She wore jeans and a neon-pink T-shirt. Pink lip gloss shimmered on her lips. Lucy felt a little plain in the yellow short-sleeved button-down her mother had bought.

Therese sat on the desk in front of Lucy, her butt on the desktop and her feet in the seat. She tapped her fingers on the glossy magazine on her lap and stared at Lucy for a long moment. For her part, Lucy just blinked at her, unsure of where to look or what to say. Therese had six inches on Lucy to go along with their three-year age difference, and Lucy wasn't so sure she'd do as well in a fight against Therese as she had against Angela.

Therese opened her mouth to speak, but then they all heard footsteps coming down the hall. The boy put his head down on his desk with the wreckage of failed flights all around him. The LaLas slipped back into their seats. Lucy straightened in her chair, but Therese didn't move from where she sat on the desk. She kept her head down like she was completely absorbed in the magazine, the tips of her braids dusting the pages as she turned them.

"Therese, take a seat." It was Miss Winthrop, the substitute teacher who taught freshman and sophomore English. She didn't look much older than the seniors who walked the halls. Every day she wore her dark-blonde hair in fat curls that covered her shoulders and a watch set in a big silver-bangle bracelet that slid up and down her arm.

"Therese," Miss Winthrop said. Therese didn't acknowledge her.

Lucy whispered, "Therese?"

Therese glanced up from the page and winked at Lucy. Slowly, she stretched one denim-clad leg out, then placed her booted foot on the floor. She sat at the desk the correct way and went back to her magazine. The LaLas giggled. They reminded Lucy of the Siamese cats in *Lady and the Tramp*, so terribly happy when others suffered.

"Thank you," Miss Winthrop said, her voice hard. "Now we all know why you're here. I hope you've been behaving yourselves. We have"—she looked at her watch—"another forty minutes together, and then you're free to go."

Therese pulled gum from her pocket, unfolded it from its silver wrapper, put it in her mouth, and proceeded to pop it loudly. Lucy saw Miss Winthrop narrow her eyes. "Therese, is your homework finished?"

"Sure." Therese flipped another page.

"So your book report is finished for my class?"

"Yep, it's all up here, Elaine," Therese said, tapping her temple. She said Miss Winthrop's name as if she had a right to. Like they were friends.

"Therese, come with me," Miss Winthrop said, her hands clenched into tight fists at her sides. Therese hopped up from her seat with a smile forming on her lips. She tossed the magazine onto Lucy's desk, winked again, and strutted past Miss Winthrop and out into the hall. Miss Winthrop followed her out, shutting the door behind her.

After five minutes, LaTasha got up, peeked through the window in the classroom's door, and shook her head. LaDonnia turned to Lucy and said, "Let me have the *Vogue*."

"It's Therese's," Lucy said.

"Come off it, white girl," said LaTasha. Lucy glared at her. She stood and, with the *Vogue* in one hand, tried to walk like Therese, with her head up and shoulders back. As Lucy got closer to the door, LaTasha backed up. She was taller than Lucy, most everyone was, but Lucy saw a flicker of fear, and she let a smile form. She paused in front of LaTasha, then flung open the door and walked out of the room. She heard LaTasha whisper "bitch" as the door closed behind her.

Lucy headed down the empty hallway to the bathroom; her sneakers near silent on the scuffed floor. Just as she passed the last classroom, she heard someone's hiccupping sobs. She edged close to the slightly open classroom door. She saw Therese with her back against the wall next to the blackboard, tears streaming down her face. Miss Winthrop stood close to her, one leg between Therese's parted legs, one hand on the wall and the other holding Therese's face, her thumb stroking her cheek. Lucy didn't breathe.

"You can't do this," Therese said. Her long black braids mingled with Miss Winthrop's blonde curls as she put her head down onto her shoulder.

"Therese," Miss Winthrop said. "I told you. I can't stay. They didn't extend my contract, but we have until the end of the school year. We have weeks before I go."

"Stay. You can work at another school," Therese said, her voice muffled.

"The school districts aren't hiring here. It's bad all over, honey.

We've talked about this. You have to stop this behavior. You're so smart. You're so beautiful." Lucy watched Therese lean in and kiss Miss Winthrop on the lips. Miss Winthrop's pale hands cradled Therese's face. Therese clutched at Miss Winthrop's waist, their bodies coming together, and one of them, Lucy couldn't tell which, let out a low moan. Lucy gasped and ducked away, nearly tripping over her own feet as she ran around the corner and into the safety of the bathroom.

Lucy gripped one of the white porcelain sinks in front of the wall-mounted mirror and tried to breathe slowly. Blood pounded in her ears. Lucy touched her own lips and wondered what it'd be like to kiss another girl. Her kissing experience was minimal. Leroy was the boy she had liked all of eighth grade, but he'd been going with another girl. But that had ended with the school year, and come summer, at a fair, Lucy found herself standing in line with Leroy for the Ferris wheel. They'd shared a carriage, and when they lurched to a stop near the top of the ride, Leroy had leaned over and kissed her. She remembered grabbing his arms and gripping tightly, as if she was going to push him away when all she wanted was to pull him closer. She remembered touching her tongue to his lips and how rough they'd felt. She remembered the firm curve of his biceps under her sweating palms. They'd parted when the ride jerked to a start again, and each of them looked away, trying to act as if the kiss hadn't been the highlight of their summer. Now he was a freshman at another school, and she was hiding out in the girls' bathroom.

A few minutes later, the door to the bathroom burst open, and Therese was there, frowning at Lucy. Lucy turned on the faucet and began washing her hands. Therese let the door close behind her. She walked up to the sink next to Lucy, dropped her tote bag on the floor, and leaned back against the sink with her arms folded across her chest.

"I know you saw," she said. She didn't sound angry.

"I won't say anything," Lucy said.

"I know you won't," Therese said. Lucy heard the threat and envisioned her end, laid out cold on the floor of the bathroom, Therese standing over her, her face blank, and the LaLas laughing and orchestrating a viewing of Lucy's body under a sign that said Lucille Jones 4 Loser Queen. Popularity status: DOA. Teasability: Astronomical.

Therese turned around to look at her reflection. She touched the puffiness under her eyes with her fingertips. She reapplied her lip gloss, smacking and puckering her lips. Lucy wondered if Miss Winthrop's lips shimmered now. Lucy could see where tears had dried on Therese's face. Lucy was so much lighter than Therese and not nearly as pretty. Therese put her hands under the faucet and delicately patted water against her cheeks.

"I heard about you and Angela. Her mother made her transfer schools," Therese said.

"Oh," was all Lucy could manage.

"Yeah, oh," Therese laughed. "Nice job getting rid of her. You know, they say Coach Daniels had to pull you off her. Guess Angela didn't know what she was getting into when she took you on, did she?"

"She was always trying to start something with me. I don't know why."

"Don't you?" Therese said and reached out to finger one of Lucy's braids. Lucy managed not to flinch. "She was jealous."

"Of what?"

"You don't have a clue how pretty you are. All this long, thick hair, plus you're gonna get taller any day now, and that weight you're carrying is gonna drift to all the right places, and when all those things line up, you're gonna be a knockout. Another year. You'll see."

"I doubt it," Lucy said.

"You'll see," Therese said, and Lucy wanted to believe her. She wanted Therese to be a friend. She wanted to bask in her aura of coolness.

"Hey, you ever think of cutting your hair?" Therese pulled a pack of cigarettes from her bag and picked up the *Vogue* from where Lucy had set it down on the sink's edge. She shook out a cigarette, lit it, and leaned back against the sink again, flipping through pages until she found what she wanted. She turned the magazine to Lucy. "You could absolutely wear your hair like this. You'd be adorable."

Lucy reached for the magazine. The pictures on the two pages were of models in 1920s-style flapper clothes. The model Therese pointed at wore her hair in a short, bobbed style with just a hint of wave in it. She was thin and angular with her eyes ringed with black eyeliner and wore a shimmering dress that caught the light. She had a drink in her hand, and her smile was wide and bright.

"I couldn't cut my hair like that. My mom would never let me."

"You always do what your mom says?" Therese exhaled a long stream of smoke toward the ceiling, then looked at Lucy with a smile on her face that said, You and me could have some fun.

———•—•———

At lunch the next day, Therese appeared at Lucy's table and said, "Come on." Therese was ditching some class, Lucy was sure of it, but she felt honored to be seen with Therese. Everyone looked at Therese with some sort of awe or at least respect. Lucy followed her out the side doors to the back of the very school where all the seniors and juniors held court. Overlooking the back- baseball field, the area consisted of one stolen cafeteria table and a stack of mats from the weight room. Therese led Lucy past several small groups of seniors to the table and introduced Lucy to her friends, a couple of girls and one named April, a girl with bad acne across her forehead, but with the loveliest brown eyes Lucy had ever seen. April patted the table next to where she sat, and Lucy hopped up beside her.

"So how did you two meet?" April asked.

"I told you, detention," Therese said.

"Can't I hear it from her, Therese?" April turned to Lucy and smiled.

"Detention," Lucy said. She glanced from April to Therese to April again, feeling like she was missing something. Therese frowned.

"So you're the one who fought Angela?"

Lucy nodded.

"We didn't get along with her really," April said, tapping the end of her cigarette into an empty Tab can.

"Hey, are you gonna help Therese get out of the tenth grade?" one girl asked.

Therese rolled her eyes. "I don't need any help."

"And yet, you flunked. Seriously, how did you fail art class?" All the girls giggled, and Lucy started to join in until she saw Therese's face twist into a scowl.

The bell rang. The girls started to pack their things. April patted Therese on the shoulder. "You know we're just playing," she said.

Lucy grabbed her backpack and stood to leave, but Therese said, "Stay and hang out." Lucy had never ditched before. In fact, her next class was math, her favorite subject, but that day, and the rest of that week, Lucy ditched with Therese. Each day Therese would come find Lucy in the cafeteria and bring her to sit amongst the older girls. Lucy listened to them talk about the senior boys, even Therese did, and Lucy got the impression that no one knew about Miss Winthrop. The girls talked about what colleges their parents wanted them to attend and who was going to the lake that weekend.

On Friday, detention was back in session. Lucy and the others sat in the auditorium watching rehearsals of *West Side Story*. On the stage, Mrs. Gould, their warden for the afternoon, was trying to get an adequate rehearsal out of her junior drama class.

They were supposed to do homework, and Lucy was, but Therese sat next to her flipping pages in the most recent issue of *Jet*, one with Janet Jackson on the cover, and pointing out hairstyles she liked. They had their feet on the backs of the wooden seats in front of them. Behind them, the boy with the airplanes seemed to have fallen asleep listening to his Walkman. Lucy caught herself humming along to the sound of New Edition's "If It Isn't Love" leaking from his headphones.

The LaLas were in the second row. They turned around occasionally, trying to catch Therese's attention, but she never looked at them. Therese kept showing Lucy pictures until she stopped writing her paper and focused on Therese. They traded thoughts on hair extensions versus natural, short versus long. Therese was adamant Lucy cut her hair.

"You would be so cute."

"I'd be dead," Lucy said.

"Your hair'd grow back quick, though. You have good hair. You don't do anything to it, do you? Just shampoo and conditioner, right?" Therese said. "You and Miss Winthrop both have good hair."

"Hers is nice. Nicer than mine," Lucy said, thinking of the twist of curls that cascaded down Miss Winthrop's back. "But she's blonde. So much better than my brown hair."

"She colors her hair. I helped her dye it once. But it's still good hair."

Lucy wondered how long Miss Winthrop and Therese had been seeing each other. Lucy said, "Really? It looks natural. Yours is nice too." She reached out touch Therese's long, thin braids.

"It's okay." Therese watched the people on the stage.

"You know I could help you with your English homework if you wanted," Lucy said. Midterm reports would be coming out the next week, and Lucy knew Therese was worried about her grades. She really didn't want to be a sophomore again. Therese's mouth dipped into a frown.

"I don't need a freshman's help to do my homework, Lucy."

"Okay, just thought I'd offer." Lucy slunk lower in her chair and went back to doing her homework.

Therese raised her hand. "Mrs. Gould, can I go to the bathroom, please?" Therese nudged Lucy with her knee.

Lucy said, "Me, too. Please."

Mrs. Gould turned from her stage instruction. "Go." When the LaLas tried to go with them, she told them they had to wait.

In the bathroom, Lucy held Therese's tote bag while Therese lit her cigarette and then took apart one of Lucy's braids, fanning the still-wet strands out and combing her fingers through her hair. "See, if we cut it to right here," Therese said, tapping Lucy's shoulder, "I bet it'll curl up to just below your chin." Lucy squinted at her reflection in the water-spotted mirror. She could sort of see what Therese was suggesting.

"You'd cut it for me?" Lucy said, hoping they were over her stupid homework offer.

"Sure," Therese said with a smile.

"I'd get in trouble."

"So tell your mom someone cut your hair at school. She'll be upset, but it'll be done."

Lucy handed Therese her bag and began to rebraid her hair. "My mom would be down here screaming at Mr. Allegretti. She'd have the PTA, the church, and the local news camped out on the principal's lawn at home if something like that happened to me. I'd have to tell her you did it, and you could be expelled."

Therese considered this, her nails tapping on the edge of the sink. "Maybe."

"Maybe? That a huge risk, don't you think?" Lucy couldn't imagine what her mother would do if she was ever expelled. Lucy thought it would involve prison for herself or her mother. She twisted the elastic band around the end of her braid. She tugged both braids and smoothed the hair back from her forehead, checking for evenness between them.

"Some risks are worth it. What are you gonna give me for doing this for you?" Therese said.

"Give you?" Lucy frowned.

"Payment, white girl. Money?"

"I don't have any money."

"Your parents do. Do they smoke?"

"My dad," Lucy said. Her voice sounded distant and small in the empty bathroom—a little girl's voice.

"I want cigarettes and money. Say forty dollars. Then I'll take the blame for cutting your hair. It's all risky, Lucy, but what's it worth to you?" The bright orange dot of the cigarette's end bounced when Therese smiled at her. Therese pulled the cigarette from her lips and licked them once. Lucy thought of Miss Winthrop kissing those lips.

"Therese, what's it like kissing Miss Winthrop?"

Therese went still for a moment, then cut Lucy a look that seemed to say Lucy had gone too far, stepped over some invisible boundary line. Then Therese shrugged. "It's kissing. It's good," she said. Therese put the cigarette out in the sink, picked up her bag, and gripped the straps tightly in her fists as if she was struggling with it. Then she closed her eyes, and her face relaxed. She sighed and said, "It's like holding on and letting go. It's better than everything."

———•◦•———

Lucy spent that Saturday on edge. She did her chores early and kept to her room with the copy of *Vogue* that Therese had sent home with her. She studied it and imagined her parents talking in their bedroom after she came home with shorter hair. Their hushed voices trickling down the hallway to her room, thick with concern. Should we take her out of school? her mother would ask. Private school? her father would wonder, putting his cigarette out in the ashtray on the nightstand. We can't afford it, her mother would say, unhappiness hanging in the air in competition with the lingering cigarette smoke. We could swing it, her father would say to make her mother happy. He would work more. They would both work more. No, Lucy decided, she wouldn't do it. She went to bed that night haunted by the look of disappointment she knew her mother's face would wear.

But Sunday night, Lucy stood in front of her dresser mirror, folded the ends of her hair up, and pinned it back with a wide barrette so she could see herself with short hair like the model Therese had shown her. Lucy imagined dark eyeliner around her eyes, her arms thin and the baby weight all dissolved into the new figure of a woman, of a sophomore. Lucy tilted her chin upward to elongate her neck. Oh, she could see her, that other self, right there in the mirror. That was a cool Lucy. Any day now, she'd be that girl, just like Therese had said.

When she was sure her parents were in their bedrooms for the night, Lucy moved silently down the hall, avoiding the spot that creaked and not turning on a single light as she went. Nervousness had her fumbling her way until she reached the bookcase in the living room. Her mother hid the cigarettes from her father in an effort to get him to cut back on them. This week they were behind worn copies of fairytales and King Arthur stories on the low bookshelf next to her mother's chair. The carton had five packs in it still. She removed one, lifted the hem of her *Jem and the Holograms* nightgown up, and slid the pack behind the waistband of her underwear, making sure it was snug against her hip, and then she replaced the books.

Her father's wallet was by the front door in the misshapen bowl Lucy had given him for Father's Day when she eight. She shifted her fingers in between and over the pieces of paper in her father's wallet, taking the first things that felt like money. With that last bit of theft done, and she knew it was theft, felt the weight of it settle on her, she crept back down the hall to her bedroom.

In the moonlight that spilled through her bedroom window, Lucy inspected the money in her hand. She'd grabbed a ten and a twenty. It'd have to do. There was no going back now. She removed the cigarettes from her underwear, pulled the tab to unwrap the cellophane from the top of the pack, and folded the money in half, then in half again, and slipped the bill down between the pack and the plastic wrapper. She put the cigarettes and the money in her pencil pouch and zipped it all away in her backpack.

In her dreams, they caught her leaving the house with the cigarettes. All her hair fell out at the breakfast table. Her nose grew Pinocchio-style when her mother asked her what she had planned for school that day. It was all ridiculous. Her mother would already be gone to work when Lucy left for school. Her father would still be asleep. They trusted Lucy to get herself going in the morning. They trusted Lucy, period.

At school the next day, there was talk in the halls about Miss Winthrop. Mrs. Dunlop was back early from her maternity leave, and Miss Winthrop was gone, effective immediately. Lucy looked for Therese in the hallways. On her way to fifth period, Lucy spotted Therese turning down another hall. Lucy sprinted after, knocking into people, apologizing as she went. The final bell for class rang, the hallways emptied, and Therese was gone. Lucy was late to math, and after ditching, she was behind in her homework, but still, she wandered the hallways looking for Therese, peeking into classroom windows and calling for Therese in a quiet voice. After five minutes, she gave up. She figured by the time she made it up the two flights of stairs she'd be a full ten minutes late for class. She was already forming plausible excuses when Therese stepped out from the recessed alcove where the bathrooms were. They looked at each other. Therese disappeared into the bathroom, and Lucy followed.

Therese was staring at her reflection in the water-spotted mirror over the sinks. Her eyes were red rimmed. Lucy noticed she was wearing Miss Winthrop's silver-bangle watch.

"I'm not staying, so if you want to do this, let's do it now." Her voice was low and miserable.

"Okay." Lucy fumbled in her backpack. Her hands shook. She thought she should say something to make Therese feel better. The bathroom they were in had no windows. The tiles seemed to glow yellow under the fluorescent lights. From her backpack, Lucy pulled the cigarettes, money, and Therese's *Vogue*, handing them all over to Therese. Therese slipped the money from the side of the pack, shoved it into her tight jeans pocket without counting it, and put the cigarettes next to a faucet.

Lucy tried again. "Therese, I'm sorry she's gone."

Therese wouldn't look at her. Lucy stood next to Therese and looked at her reflection in the mirror, hoping to convey how sorry she felt for the other girl. Lucy thought she understood what the absence of Miss Winthrop must feel like to Therese. She thought of Leroy in his school across town and the press of his lips against her own. At least Therese wouldn't have to see Miss Winthrop with another girl like Lucy had had to watch Leroy in eighth grade.

Therese opened the magazine and found the page with the model on it. She balanced the magazine on the edge of the sink.

"Look straight ahead," Therese said, stepping behind Lucy and adjusting her head in the mirror. "Keep it here, or it'll be shorter than we want." She went back to her bag and pulled out scissors and set them on the sink's edge.

"You remind me of Elaine," Therese said. She took up the end of Lucy's braid with her left hand and began winding the hair around her hand, tugging hard with each successive loop of hair. "She's smart like you are. Too smart. She thinks I need help too. She thinks I need more than she can give me. All I needed was her, though."

"Therese, you're hurting me," Lucy said.

"Don't be a baby." Therese took up the scissors with her right hand. Lucy saw something dark and angry on her face.

"I'm not a baby, Therese. Just stop," Lucy said, her voice was just this side of a whine. Therese yanked on her braid. Lucy yelped in pain.

"Shut up and hold still."

"No," Lucy said, afraid now. Lucy pulled away from Therese, backing up and pushing at Therese. Therese followed, her hand pulling harder now, the scissors edging closer.

"Stop it. Or I'll cut you," Therese said.

The girls turned in a circle, Lucy trying to pull away and Therese trying to stop her. Their voices rose until Therese yelled, "Hold still" again and forced Lucy down onto her knees with her fist hard against the side of Lucy's head. Fat tears ran down Lucy's face as the scissors made their first cut just above Therese's knuckles.

"No," Lucy said, her voice just a whisper.

With the last snip of the scissors, the length of hair pulled away from Lucy, and Therese straightened. "There. One side down and one to go. That wasn't so bad, now was it?" she said.

The bathroom door opened, and Mrs. Gould walked in on the tableau, Therese with scissors in her right hand, a thick braid of hair in her left hanging like meat in a butcher's case, and Lucy on her knees sobbing, her face in her hands.

"Girls, what exactly is going on here?" Mrs. Gould asked, looking from one girl to the other.

Therese looked at Lucy crying and said, "She wanted me to do it."

Lucy tried to stifle her sobs. The bathroom air was cool on her neck. Her head felt lopsided without the weight of her hair on her right side. What was left of her braid began to unravel as she stood up. She looked at herself in the mirror. A different Lucy stared back. A Lucy she didn't recognize. One that didn't match any version she had imagined. Lucy wiped at the tears on her face.

"Come with me," Mrs. Gould said.

Mrs. Gould took the scissors and reached for the curl of braid still wrapped around Therese's hand, but Therese shoved it at Lucy, who took it and clutched it against her torso.

"It's what you wanted," Therese said. *Vogue* lay discarded on the floor. Therese picked it up as she picked up her bag off the floor. She glared at Lucy, her arms folded, her eyes shiny with tears of her own.

Outside the principal's office, they sat in the hardback chairs not looking at each other. Lucy's mother arrived first and gasped when she saw Lucy's hair.

"Baby," her mother said, and pulled Lucy to her chest. Out of the corner of her eye, Lucy could see Therese watching them. Studying them like Lucy had studied the girls in *Vogue*, trying to figure out how to become like them.

Our Man Julian

Two weeks after his diagnosis, Julian strode into the bank, the tip of his cane clacking on the marble tiles. He nodded at the security guard, a man in his mid-fifties with a mean-looking gun holstered on his hip. All guns looked mean to Julian. They were designed to inflict pain, to cause fear. Julian understood their uses. You couldn't be black and have lived through Jim Crow without understanding the purpose of a gun.

Julian was an entertainer. His purpose was to try to make his audience understand those unlike themselves. He'd played thugs, wife-beaters, doctors, technicians, mechanics—and quite a few pimps. He'd been the dead body in the room too. Now he would be the old black man trying to open a checking account. He was harmless, armed with nothing more dangerous than his cane and two cell phones.

Julian had reached the peak of his talent in the seventies acting in movies, the kind they called blaxploitation. He never became a star like Richard Roundtree or Pam Grier, but he'd done okay. He'd made some money—more from the behind-the-scenes deals he cut than the movie roles, but he'd done well enough to put away a nice amount and still send money home to his mother. The rest of the money went to fueling his recreational fun.

And he'd had fun. He'd been a fool and reckless, he'd learned to admit that much. After 1973, he sent a large portion of his money to the women who were pregnant with his children.

There was Gwen, who had refused the money, saying she didn't need it or him. But Julian insisted on it, telling her that once her family found out that their pretty blonde daughter was carrying a black man's child, they wouldn't be so accommodating of her situation. He'd been right, and she hated him all the more for it. She was furious with him and heartbroken when she'd found about the other impending baby.

The other woman, Leandra, was a stone-cold woman, no doubt about that. She had a calmer head. She took the money and promised to give the child his last name, Morningside. Julian had seen the name written on the side of a building the day the bus he was on pulled into LA. He'd loved the idea of it.

The morning side of life. The good side. Everything looks better in the morning, he'd thought. He changed his name that day from Adams, respectable but common, to Morningside. At his first audition, he introduced himself as Julian Morningside.

———— •◆• ————

The day after Julian's doctor visit was a Tuesday, and as always, his friend Maxwell showed up to play dominos and drink beer. Julian hadn't wanted the company and almost called to cancel but forgot to call. His head was filled with images of his daughters' faces and figuring out insurance co-pays. Just the initial outlay of money required to possibly save his life would wipe out the last of his savings.

When Julian opened the door, the sight of Maxwell, all of five foot five in height, scowling up at him through the fronds of one of Julian's larger plants killed the lie on his tongue. Maxwell always had a comment about Julian's front yard, and hearing the man grumble was often the best part of the visit.

"Why would you have plants that look like they want to eat you?" Maxwell said, giving the offending plant—known as Delicious Monster because of the fruit it bore and the prehistoric widths of its leaves—side-eye as he pushed past it to enter the house. "Fucking Jurassic Park shit."

Julian liked the feeling of isolation the plants gave the house. They muffled the sound of the freeway that flowed through the tunnel beneath the neighborhood and exited ten yards over from his place. The whole front yard was filled with trees and plants with massive leaves and fronds that hid the front of the house. Julian had spent quite a bit on the plants a decade ago. Now the plants had matured, and once a month, the son of the guy who had sold him the plants stopped by to check on them.

Maxwell was a sore loser, but he liked to talk. He talked about his son and his ex-wife and Jasmine, the pregnant girlfriend, and how all of them were expensive: college, alimony, gifts. "They all want a piece of me, man. I just want be old."

Julian laughed at him. "Your son calls you three times a week like you're a church he needs to visit to keep himself on the straight and narrow. He loves you and hates that he has to be a better man than you. You are your own problem."

Maxwell shrugged. "Like you ain't done nothing."

"I have daughters, one who wants nothing to do with me and the other who would never side against her to be nearer me. All I want is to have something to give them when I pass. Damn housing bubble. This place won't be worth anything by the time it's theirs."

"What I'm saying is that you don't have the kind of monthly dues I have. I live in a crappy apartment. You got the *Land of the Lost* in your front yard and a badass jacuzzi in your back yard." Maxwell slapped his domino down, completing his house and ending the game.

Between the first cancer treatment and the IRS threatening jail for overdue taxes, Julian had run through the bulk of his savings five years ago. He was lucky the girls hadn't wanted him to pay for college. He was afraid of becoming a burden to them. He was sure that Thessaly, despite her disappointment in him, would take it upon herself to make sure he was cared for, even if it meant doing it herself. Julietta, his insider, was the one who sent him pictures once a year. When she was little, she told him when her mother was thinking about cutting him off from her or taking him back to court. Julietta would follow Thessaly's lead.

He was proud of his girls. Their mothers had effectively steered them away from acting and Hollywood. His daughters lived in Vegas. Julietta worked as a secretary for a lawyer, and Thessaly was a civil engineer. He occasionally wondered if Etta was really a showgirl in one of those shows where they only wore rhinestones and heels and just couldn't bear to tell him the truth. She was tall enough for it: five foot ten in her bare feet.

For Thessaly, it was her mother's genes that held her height back. At barely five foot two, she'd always been sensitive about people looking down at her. But she had her mother's coloring—her skin a high golden brown and her eyes a very light brown, attributes that had drawn boys to her like moths when she was in high school and college.

But she had rules, and boys who only played football or baseball didn't interest her. He wondered now if Thessaly had love in her life. Etta would regale him with her dating stories, but all he heard about

Thessaly was how many hours she put in at work, and some large public works project she headed up. He wondered if engineering fed some part of her like making movies had fed him when he was younger. Even if it did, Thessaly would need love, companionship in her later years. It took Julian decades to figure that out for himself. Now he only had Maxwell.

"You know, I might have something for you," Maxwell said now as he mixed the tiles, then divvied them up between them. "I was going to do it, but Jasmine is due any day now, and she swears she doesn't want me there. But I just know it's gonna happen soon, and I gotta be there for the newest Robison to be born."

After Maxwell left, Julian stood at the end of his driveway looking down at the note he'd been given with a room number and address for a motel in La Jolla. Maxwell wouldn't tell him what the "something" might be. Julian let his gaze wander to the end of the street, where a chain-link fence was all that stood to stop a fall onto the freeway. When they were little, the girls would stand there and loop their skinny fingers through the chain-link fence. He'd walked up behind them once and listened to them talk as they watched the cars and wondered aloud where they thought the drivers were heading. Then where they would go when they were old enough.

"Alaska," Thessaly offered.

"Nah, Antarctica," Julietta insisted.

"I think we'd need an icebreaker to get there," Thessaly said. She was the detailer. Etta would dream big, and Thessaly would research and plan.

"Is that a boat?"

"A ship."

"A real big one?" Julietta asked.

"Not sure."

"Sounds like a big ship."

"We can check the *Britannica* in Daddy's house."

Etta shrugged. "But you'll come with me?"

"Yep. First Antarctica, then Alaska, okay?"

"Okay."

In his head, they were always this age, not more than six—innocent and, above all, happy to see him every visit. He'd let them down over the years. Telling them he was coming for a visit, then letting something change his plans (usually it was a woman, for a couple years it was stuff harder to shake).

But he kept to the custody schedule no matter what: Christmas breaks on the odd years and spring breaks on the evens, and the month of July every year. He always tried to be sober for their visits. He never brought a woman home during his time with them. The three of them spent a lot of happy times on this block. Then they grew up, and his best wasn't good enough to keep them from being angry about his choices. Their mothers had gone on, married other people, and provided his girls with better lives than he had. Julian needed to leave them something, and the only thing he had was the house. The idea of his death didn't faze him, but knowing he could go and leave them nothing broke his heart. Without a better plan, he'd end up mortgaging it to afford the hospital bills. He needed another option.

———— •●• ————

The man on the other side of the motel door was in his late twenties. Michael was barrel-chested, had a shaved head and a neck tattoo of something Julian couldn't quite make out. Its curved lines inched up over the collar of his white button-down shirt and reminded Julian of whales breaching water. Last time he'd seen whales, the girls had been ten or eleven, and they'd all been on a boat together, each girl gripping one of his hands and grinning so hard he thought their faces would never recover.

"You're Julian. Come in."

Julian stepped into the room and glanced around. Bed, dresser, table with two chairs, and one closed door where the bathroom should be. Julian didn't think they were actually alone. Michael sat on the edge of the bed. "You were in *Shaft*."

Julian frowned. Few ever recognized him, none as young as the light-skinned boy in front of him.

"Yeah, Max mentioned you were some big-time actor. Looked you up, saw you were in *Shaft*, and I had to watch that shit again. I haven't seen that since I was little. You know when they'd show the real violent stuff on late-late night? My mom, she worked night shift. I'd spend the whole night watching TV and listening to people fight and fuck in the apartment next door."

"*Shaft* was a long time ago." It'd been a small role. He'd been on screen all of five minutes before he died, but he hadn't ended up on the editing room floor, so it counted.

"Sure was. Look, I need someone to go somewhere and tell me when a certain man shows up. Simple as that."

"Simple."

"Simple, man."

Julian sighed. He sat in one of the chairs and arranged his long limbs more comfortably. "I can do that. It's hardly a stretch of acting skills. Details are needed though."

"If I tell you, you're in. Stand me up and you better be dead."

Julian gave a little nod. Michael said, "Rigby." And the door to the bathroom opened. A man—young like Michael but white—emerged. He was short, thin with a head of blond hair in desperate need of a cut. He rolled a toothpick back and forth between his lips while he looked at Julian.

"He in?" Rigby asked.

"He is. Julian, this is Rigby. We all are gonna rob a bank."

Julian stood up.

Rigby laughed and said, "Relax, old man, we aren't doing it today."

Julian hadn't stood up because he'd been shocked by the news of their goal. It was because of the idea that came to him at that very moment. The lightning strike. His salvation. His solution. If they didn't die in this endeavor, which he knew was likely, prison was now a destination between him and his imminent death. In prison, he'd be treated for his cancer until the very end. His girls wouldn't have to spend a dime or a minute of time on him. All he had to worry about was the house. He had to make sure they got it and not the state.

"How much is my cut?" Julian wanted to know, settling again in the chair. The idea twisted around in his head.

"Ten grand. Half up front."

"I need all it now." Michael's square jaw shifted, but he said nothing. Julian said, "Look if this goes as you plan it. No big deal. But if anything goes off plan, maybe I don't come back. I have debts to settle."

Rigby said, "Bullshit."

"And I need to know how much time I have before this happens."

Rigby paced. Michael looked at Julian for a long moment. "At least a week, maybe more."

———•◦•———

Julian called Julietta that night. Her voice was heavy with sleep when she answered.

"Dad? You okay?"

Julian said, "I sure am, now that I'm talking to you."

She giggled and asked him to hold on. He listened to her get out of bed. She got back on the phone, and they discussed nothing. The weather. New shoes she bought. Her sister's desire for a dog. Then Julian came to the point of his call.

"I need . . . no, I want to sign over the house to the both of you."

"What's wrong?" Her voice fluttered up high.

"Etta, relax. Nothing's wrong. I'm old, honey, I won't be here forever."

"Daddy," she said.

"I want you girls to have this house. I bought it for you two anyway. A place where we could all be together. We had good times here, didn't we?" Julian heard her sniffle. "Sweetheart, I just want you girls to have this place. Inheritance taxes might keep it from you."

"It's just a house, Daddy. We want you." Etta sighed. "But I'll get her to sign whatever you need."

Three days later, he registered the signed and notarized document with the state. The house was theirs. That night he slept better than he had in years.

———•◦•———

Julian entered the bank five minutes after it opened. He signed his name and waited in one of three almost-comfortable upholstered chairs for customer service to call his name.

The pain in his side was not constant, but it was letting him know it was there; slowly growing, still unchecked, an advancing army in his undefended body. There would be surgery, then chemotherapy. He'd barely survived the last bout with cancer, and he'd been fit and sober then. Sixty-five years old but in better shape, more like a man of fifty, his doctor had said. He spent three days in a coma after his colon surgery. They didn't know why he didn't wake straight away. Then they had to stop the chemo because he wasn't strong enough for it. They'd wait. Do more tests. He'd start feeling like a person again, and then it would begin again. Months and months of see-sawing the medications trying to figure out how to save him. He didn't look forward to doing it again.

Julian was pulled from his thoughts by a soft voice. "Mr. Morningside?"

The woman—a beautiful woman by his quick estimation, olive skinned, dark hair, and darker eyes—watched him closely as he rose. He saw the look, and he cursed himself. He was so rarely recognized these days, but she was near his age bracket—at least within fifteen years of him, he thought. She'd be the right age to have seen his movies when they were big. Some people remembered him as the young black cop who died at Sidney Poitier's feet in *They Call Me Mister Tibbs!* Most remembered him as the second pimp Pam Grier shoots for getting her sister hooked on heroin in *Coffy*. Few actually knew his name though. He extended his hand to her. "That's me."

Her hand was soft and cool to the touch. He released her, but she held on a moment longer as she looked at his face. She invited him to have a seat in her cubicle. The sway of her hips was impressive. He watched one hip swing her skirt close to the edge of the desk, and the next step brought her skirt brushing against the fabric-covered wall of the cubicle. He couldn't tell if she walked that way naturally or if she was turning it up for him.

"You don't remember me, do you?" She sat down across from him with a smirk on her face.

"How long ago are we talking?" He leaned his cane against her desk.

"The wrap party for *Night in the City*."

Julian blinked. That'd been his movie. A retelling of *Hamlet*. It was going to be his breakout role. He'd had two kids on the way, and the world, he thought, was finally opening up for him as an actor.

Deep down in the secret corners of his heart, he'd harbored the wish to be as good as Sidney Poitier, his one great idol. *Night in the City* was going to make him something. Then the NAACP went on record deploring blaxploitation pictures, and the money dried up for independent distribution, and no studio would buy it after. Suddenly every studio was wary of movies with all black casts. But all that disappointment would come later, and the wrap party that night was a blur of bodies and alcohol and drugs, and Julian had been king of it.

"Sorry, I don't. I mean I was pretty full of myself back then. I probably spent a lot of time with a lot of girls—women, I mean, back then." Julian winced.

She laughed. "It's fine. You were very kind to me. We made out for a little bit, and then you were off with another girl, and I floated out of there higher than any drug could've made me that night. I was twenty-two, and you were a fine-looking actor."

"Did I at least get your name back then?"

"I don't remember. But let's do this: Hello, Mr. Morningside. My name is Sonia Landry, what can Bank West do for you today?"

She told him about the accounts available, interest versus no interest, and the fees that would apply. Her scent—lavender and something else, something earthy—drifted across the desk to him, making him lean closer. Each time he looked up from the brochure in front of him, he found her watching him steadily. Julian forgot himself. He mentioned Thessaly's childhood obsession with counting. Then they were discussing kids.

"Do you have pictures? I have a son, Hector."

Julian removed his phone from his inner jacket pocket and shuffled through the photos to find the picture Etta sent him last New Year's Eve. She and Thessaly dressed up in short skirts, heels, and were sparkling from head to toe. He handed Sonia the phone.

She looked closely at the photo, then handed the phone back. "They're beautiful."

"Like I said, I was full of myself back then. I did a lot of things I shouldn't have, but I was lucky. I have my girls."

Julian had completely forgotten his task until a man called out "good morning" to Sonia and she glanced up and waved. "Morning, Mr. Alvarez."

Julian watched the man go by. He shook himself and carefully put in the number and sent a text message. He slipped the phone back into his jacket pocket. "Now show me your Hector."

A minute later, four masked men exploded through the front door before she could show him the picture of her son. "Nobody move!"

Two of the masked men pulled the tellers out from behind their counter. Rigby, recognizable by the tuft of blond hair that stuck out beyond the edge of his mask, yanked one teller over the counter by the front of his shirt and deposited him nose first onto the floor. A spray of blood fanned out across the white marble.

The masked men herded everyone into sitting positions around the lobby desks. One of them yanked the pens off their chains, scattering withdrawal and deposit slips. They demanded their cell phones. The leader—Julian assumed it was Michael—came to him with his hand out, and Julian hesitated. Then he reached into his pants pocket and pulled out the little black phone Michael had given him just days before. Julian had made a mistake. He'd sent the text from the wrong phone. Michael knew it and made a point of smashing the phone with his heel in front of Julian, his eyes on him hard.

Michael turned and pointed at Alvarez, who was crouching down with the tellers. Rigby and another masked man descended on Alvarez, yanking him up by his arms. He begged to be left alone. The man's face had gone a florid red. His eyes bulged. He screamed when

Rigby hit him in the face and bloodied his nose. The male tellers turned their heads away. The female tellers closed their eyes.

The security guard moved away from the others, stupidly rose to his knees, and said, "Hey, stop! He'll do what you want." Rigby let go of Alvarez and walked over to the guard. The guard leaned back as Rigby came closer. The guard's right hand drifted toward his ankle.

The guard was right in front of where Julian had an arm locked around Sonia. She was chanting "Ohgodohgodohgod" in a whisper into his shoulder. Julian tightened his grip on her.

Rigby shot the guard in the head.

The sound reverberated off the floor and the walls, followed quickly by a scream from one of the tellers. Michael yelled at him to stop. Told everyone to keep cool and they'd go home. Then he and the other masked men walked and dragged Alvarez down through the side door and out of view, leaving Rigby to watch over them.

Rigby paced around them. Finger on the trigger of his gun. Each time his circuit brought him in front of Julian, he paused, making sure he made eye contact with him. Sonia didn't see. The others kept their heads down. No one wanted to see anything. Julian grew convinced with each revolution that Rigby would never let him go when the job was done. Julian would never make it to prison. With Sonia in his arms, gasping into his lapel, Julian realized he didn't want to go to jail. He was sure he was going to die, but he'd be damned before he let Rigby be his grim reaper.

The guard had fallen on his back, his right leg tucked under him. Julian could just make out something against the white of the guard's sock. An ankle holster. The guard probably fancied himself a cop. Maybe thought he'd need it one day in case a repeat of the North Hollywood bank robbery happened on his watch.

Julian guessed Michael and the others had been gone for five minutes. Things would end soon. Julian told Sonia this as Rigby passed him again. She nodded. Julian patted her shoulder and let her go. She sat up on her own, hands locked in prayer, mouth still moving. Julian leaned forward, reached under the guard's pant leg and the gun free of its holster, then he pulled back, slipped the gun into his waistband, and waited for Rigby to come into view again.

Rigby stopped in front of them this time. He gestured with the gun at Sonia. "You praying, huh? Think it's gonna work for you?" He poked her in the shoulder with the gun. Sonia whimpered, but she didn't open her eyes. Julian put his shoulder against hers and stared at Rigby. Rigby pointed the gun at him, pretended to shoot the gun. He winked and walked around the desk.

Two minutes later, Michael and the other men walked out through the door. They each had a bag. Alvarez wasn't with them. "We're done. Let's roll," Michael said.

The men walked carefully around the guard, making sure to sidestep the blood and brains. Michael stood in the doorway. "Come on."

Rigby pointed his gun at everyone. "Keep your mouths shut." He turned away. Julian released the breath he'd been holding. He'd been wrong about Rigby. He was so grateful to be wrong. It was over.

Then Rigby turned back again when he was almost at the door. "You know, I think y'all need a reminder of why you shouldn't talk." He raised his gun, but Julian was already in motion, firing two shots low. One went wide. The second clipped Rigby in the leg, bringing him down. Julian extended his arm, and the third shot caught Rigby in the throat. Rigby dropped his gun, and both hands went to stop the blood. It flowed over his fingers and pooled on the floor. Michael looked at the scene from the other side of the glass doors. Then he turned and ran.

——•◆•——

The police arrived minutes later. Julian waited with Sonia, an arm wrapped around her trembling shoulders and her head resting under his chin. A detective came to talk to him again, and Sonia went with one of the EMTs. Her trembling had given way to crying, and there was little Julian could do for her. He promised to see her later.

The detective asked what happened. Julian closed his eyes for a moment, considered his daughters and the lovely Sonia. "He shot the guard and then turned his back to us. His compatriots rushed forward, yelling at him, bags in their hands. They hustled out the door. He was to be the last one through. I pulled out the guard's gun and shot him."

The detective wrote in his notebook. "He was pointing the gun at you? You were in danger at that moment?"

"I suppose I was in as much danger as the guard had been in the seconds leading up to the trigger being pulled."

The detective nodded. A few more questions and he sent Julian on his way. Julian went with the ambulance that held Sonia. Stayed with her while she called her family and explained, switching from English to Spanish and back again, what had happened. She thanked him.

"It's not a problem. Is your husband coming?"

"No husband anymore." She patted his hand.

"Can I escort you home?" he asked. She smiled and nodded.

At her apartment across town, she let him pour her a glass of wine. Then she let him into her bed. To comfort her, he told himself. He absolutely wasn't hiding.

The next morning, he woke to an empty bed and singing coming from another room. He was warm and satisfied in a way he hadn't been in years. He'd call the girls today and invite them over for a long weekend. Julietta would say maybe, and Thessaly would flat out say no, but then he thought Etta would try to cover Thessaly's rudeness and promise to come. Later, when his doorbell rang, it would be both girls on his doorstep.

He had time still. He could do right by them still. He'd bring up the cancer to them carefully, over a series of phone calls perhaps. That way they wouldn't think it was just because he was dying and afraid to be alone. He'd make sure they knew how much he loved them.

He nodded to himself and swung his legs out of Sonia's bed. In the kitchen, he kissed her cheek and set a hand on her hip. She smiled and pushed him away, telling him to go sit; she'd make him breakfast.

"How do you feel about eggs?" Sonia asked.

"Same way I feel about everything right now. I feel good about eggs."

She laughed.

The knock that came twenty minutes later didn't worry him. "Oh, that's the paper man coming for his money. Drink your coffee—and no more bacon for you," she said. She pointed a long finger at him.

He promised. As soon as she was gone, he leaned over the counter and filched another piece. From the other room, he could hear bits of conversation. Then he heard Sonia say, "Oh, he's here."

His side gave a little twinge. The cancer saying hello, he assumed. Or maybe it was something else. He heard footsteps, and they weren't Sonia's. He knew who it was.

"Good morning, Detective."

"Mr. Morningside, you weren't at home. We came to ask Ms. Landry questions about you."

"She doesn't know a thing. We'd never met before yesterday. Leave her be."

"If she's honest with us, there'll be no problems. Same goes for you." The detective rounded the breakfast bar to stand near him.

"Ask your questions then," Julian said.

Julian thought of how Sonia's warm body had curled against him the night before. But of course, someone had to get hurt. His favorite movies always ended with the main character not getting the girl. Whether she was left behind with tears in her eyes or walking away cursing the main character, someone had to get hurt. Too much was at stake. Every character needed to lose something, even if they were only on the screen for a day.

"Mr. Morningside, I was hoping you could tell me how it is the dead robber had a text message from you on his phone."

"I think it's pretty obvious how that happened," Julian said, and waited for the end he knew was coming. This was the ending he'd planned for ultimately. He would go to prison. The girls would get the house.

"Yeah, I'm going to need you to come with me, sir," the detective said.

"Just let me get my pants on." Julian walked to the bedroom, sat down heavily on the bed, and put his face in his hands.

83

You twitch and flop on the sweat-soaked bedspread and listen to the hum of the AC. The walls are thin, and you try not to make too much noise (someone may have banged on a wall or ceiling).

Between hallucinations (or during, you don't remember), you decide the motel's maid has a bad foot or leg, because when she makes her rounds, you hear a slide-thunk along with the squeaky wheels of her cart. Knock at a door, the slide-thunk moves away. Slam of a door, and it's back again, but the squeak is a straight-line sound. It goes silent, but when it returns, it always moves forward.

When you close your eyes, you think some karmic god must have the tines of a fork stuck in your gut and is twisting them slowly, making you yowl and cry like some lovesick cat. You open your eyes and your eyeballs itch.

You owe a man money. You think as often as he fucked you y'all should be even, but he claims your debt is bigger than even your sweet piece of ass is worth. So you emptied your bank account ($800) and left town (quickly).

You left behind a niceish apartment and the job that paid for everything material you could want, but fifteen years of constant pressure finally broke you. So fuck that job.

Fuck your parents too. Once they decided that you had decided getting high with him was more important, they wrote you off. Friends, if you had them, were work friends, and they're gone with the job.

Your sister—ten years younger, your confidant (your BFF)—is the only one who still calls. You tossed your phone on the way to Reno, but you can still get your voicemails. You listen briefly to his demented slobbering. He swears he'll find you, he'll kill you. You delete his and save hers. Each night you listen to her say, Come home. Stay with me. Nothing is okay, but you're okay with me. You go to sleep to those messages. She's the reason you're here now, trying to let go of the drugs and the mistake of a life you made with him. For her, you're sweating and cursing and weeping in a motel room where no one cares what you're doing as long as you pay upfront and don't burn the place down.

You've given up everything but alcohol and cigarettes. A girl needs to have something to find solace in. Marlboros and Jameson sit in a bag next to the gun you bought off some guy behind the liquor store. You took your ex–drug dealer's messages seriously. You are a woman (an addict) who thought she loved a man. You see your mistakes clearly now.

It's been enough days that, though sleep is still torturing for you, it does come at times during the day, which means you're awake at night listening to the sounds of the motel world. On one side a TV plays loudly, incessantly, from 10:00PM till 2:00AM. In the other room, there's a woman with kids. Each night, you hear them pray, then muffled laughter. You imagine them bouncing on the bed and their mother kissing them goodnight. Later, you hear her talking while pacing on the sidewalk in front of your room.

When your sister was small, you sang her to sleep each night. In the room you shared, you crooned made-up songs using words from her favorite books. "I love you so I'll eat you up like green eggs and ham" and other nonsense. She'd giggle and hum along until she fell asleep, and you'd keep going, singing softer and softer until all you could hear was her quiet breathing and the cars on the highway whipping past your house.

You believe he will find you. There is a bullet in the chamber and several in the clip. You know how to work the safety. You wait for the footsteps you don't recognize to pause in front of your door, then for someone—him—to gently test the doorknob. You sleep with a gun under your pillow because you're sure that's the only way home.

———•◦•———

You twitch and flop on the sweat-soaked bedspread and listen to the hum of the A/C. The walls are thin, and you try not to make too much noise (someone may have banged on a wall or ceiling).

Between hallucinations (or during, you don't remember), you decide the motel's maid has a bad foot or leg because when she makes her rounds, you hear a slide-thunk along with the squeaky wheels of her cart. Knock at a door, the slide-thunk moves away. Slam of a door, and it's back again, but the squeak is a straight-line sound. It goes silent, but when it returns, it always moves forward.

When you close your eyes, you think some karmic god must have the tines of a fork stuck in your gut and is twisting them slowly making you yowl and cry like some lovesick cat. You open your eyes and your eyeballs itch.

You owe a man money. You think as often as he fucked you y'all should be even, but he claims your debt is bigger than even your sweet piece of ass is worth. So you emptied your bank account ($800) and left town (quickly).

You left behind a nice-ish apartment and the job that paid for everything material you could want but 15 years of constant pressure finally broke you. So fuck that job.

Fuck your parents too. Once they decided that you had decided getting high with him was more important, they wrote you off. Friends, if you had them, were work friends and they're gone with the job.

Your sister—ten years younger, your confidant (your BFF)—is the only one who still calls. You tossed your phone on the way to Reno, but you can still get your voicemails. You listen briefly to his demented slobbering. He swears he'll find you, he'll kill you. You delete his and save hers. Each night you listen to her say, Come home. Stay with me. Nothing is okay, but you're okay with me. You go to sleep to those messages. She's the reason you're here now, trying to let go of the drugs and the mistake of a life you made with him. For her, you're sweating and cursing and weeping in a motel room where no one cares what you're doing as long as you pay upfront and don't burn the place down.

You've given up everything but alcohol and cigarettes. A girl needs to have something to find solace in. Marlboros and Jameson sit in a bag next to the gun you bought off some guy behind the liquor store. You took your ex-drug dealer's messages seriously. You are a woman (an addict) who thought she loved a man. You see your mistakes clearly now.

It's been enough days that though sleep is still torture for you, it does come at times during the day, which means you're awake at night listening to the sounds of the motel world. On one side a TV plays loudly, incessantly, from 10PM til 2AM. In the other room, there's a woman with kids. Each night, you hear them pray then muffled laughter. You imagine them bouncing on the bed and their mother kissing them goodnight. Later, you hear her talking while pacing on the sidewalk in front of your room.

When your sister was small, you sang her to sleep each night. In the room you shared, you crooned made up songs using words from her favorite books 'I love you so I'll eat you up like green eggs and ham' and other nonsense. She'd giggle and hum along until she fell asleep and you'd keep going, singing softer and softer until all you could hear was her quiet breathing and the cars on the highway whipping past your house.

You believe he will find you. There is a bullet in the chamber and several in the clip. You know how to work the safety. You wait for the footsteps you don't recognize to pause in front of your door, then for someone—him—to gently test the doorknob. You sleep with a gun under your pillow because you're sure that's the only way home.

ACKNOWLEDGEMENTS

Thank you, Shawn Cosby for always listening to my writing woes. Thank you to Sandra Ruttan and Renee Pickup. Thanks to my children who left me alone long enough to write these stories they weren't allowed to read. Thank you to my parents Teresa and Carol, Don and Earletta. Thank you, Don, Dana, Jonathan, and Lauren. I love you all.

Thank you to my teachers: Lee Barnes and Marcia Brenner and Sam Weller and Audrey Niffenegger. You all made the difference for me.

Thanks to the Bronzeville team: Danny, Allison, Dana, Julia and Hailey. You all held my hand through this journey, and I am better for it. Thank you to Crime Writers of Color for your support and to the members of Short Mystery Fiction Society.

Thank you to R, my favorite. You always make things a little better.

NIKKI DOLSON is a writer primarily of short fiction, which has been published in places like *Shotgun Honey, Tough, Thuglit,* & *Bartleby Snopes.* She's also written a novel-ish thing, *All Things Violent.*

CPSIA information can be obtained
at www.ICGtesting.com
Printed in the USA
LVHW080304200920
665889LV00001BA/6/J